MW00784908

# Wishwood

Other books by E.B. Wheeler

*The Haunting of Springett Hall*
*Born to Treason*
*No Peace with the Dawn* (with Jeffery Bateman)
*Yours, Dorothy*
*Letters from the Homefront*
*The Bone Map*
*Bootleggers & Basil*
*Utah Women: Pioneers, Poets & Politicians*

# Wishwood

E.B. Wheeler

Wishwood © 2020 E.B. Wheeler

All rights reserved. No part of this book may be reproduced in any form or by any means without permission in writing from the publisher.

This book is a work of fiction. Names, characters, places, and events in this book are either the products of the author's imagination or are used fictitiously.

ISBN: 978-1-7321631-4-0

First printing: January 2020
Published by Rowan Ridge Press, Utah
Cover and interior design © Rowan Ridge Press
Front cover photos © Vladimir Mulder; faestock

*For Spanish Dan,*
*Scourge of the battlefield*

# Chapter One

I often dreamed of home. Of the rose petal softness of the mother I had hardly known. Of the father who had been my guiding star and then deserted me. Of being embraced and cherished by gentle hearts and hands.

I dreamed of Aubrey Hall.

Then I awoke in a cold bed in Lord Blacknall's monstrous stone keep. Drafts slithered through the corridors. The bed curtains hung too close, blocking out the light of sun, moon, and candle, suffocating me.

And each time I awoke, my wedding to a stranger drew ever nearer, until finally, the inescapable day arrived.

"Oh, Lady Katherine, please don't do this!" My old nurse, Becca, cinched the laces running up the back of my bodice before blowing her nose in a handkerchief. At least, I assume it was a handkerchief. She would never use the blue silk of my wedding dress, even though it had been a gift from Lord Blacknall. "Your dear father would weep to see such a day."

I fixed my gaze on the black eagle painted on the plaster above the fireplace. Lord Blacknall's emblem watched me even in my borrowed chamber, as inescapable as the man himself. "Then he should not have left me alone."

Everyone would desert me eventually. My eyes stung for a moment, but I blinked hard to clear them. My father's position as Baron de Aubrey made me an heiress, and his recklessness left me an orphan while I was still a minor. This unhappy combination meant my person and my lands became the property of King Charles, who sold off my guardianship to the highest bidder: Lord Blacknall. Now I was the only one left to watch out for everyone at Aubrey Hall.

Becca sniffled. "Oh, my poor lamb."

Not a lamb. Lambs are fleeced or sent to the slaughter. I would not allow either. "I have to play Lord Blacknall's game until I can get Aubrey Hall out of his hands."

Becca frowned and pulled my blonde hair into a loose knot at the base of my neck, her gentle, motherly touch almost painful when I realized that I might never feel it again. "But letting Lord Blacknall sell you off to some stranger! Probably a lecherous, poxy old man."

My lips twitched at her description of my imagined groom, but I did not laugh. It might betray my nervousness. "He may be many things, but he cannot be *old*. He is another of Lord Blacknall's wards."

"But this is marriage! You should not throw it away." Becca practically stamped her foot, and here she was more than twice my age.

"Many people marry for political or economic reasons."

"I wanted better for you, my lady."

So had I.

Now, I had to put dreams of love or affection behind me. I touched the *memento mori* ring on my finger, with its skull and the date of my father's death—1628—four years earlier. In those years, the game I had learned to play was survival.

When I made no reply, Becca took the curling tongs from the fireplace. I sat on a chair by my dressing table, a beeswax candle casting a circle of warmth that did not quite reach me. Becca carefully arranged the blonde curls around my face. I sat still, surrounded by the faint scent of slightly burnt hair, my silk gown falling around me like a frozen waterfall.

She finished and fussed over my white lace collar. Unnecessary, but I let her, drifting for a pleasant moment in the memories of childhood when such acts of affection had cocooned me. I had not realized how much love had been woven through the small moments of my life until I lost it all.

Would my husband have a gentle touch?

"If only Lord Blacknall allowed me to go with you," Becca said.

If only! I almost slipped up and agreed with her, but at that moment, the heavy oak door banged open, and Lord Blacknall stepped into the room. He wore his blond mustache waxed to needle points, and his lips curved up in a self-satisfied smile. And why should he not look smug? He had won this round of our battle.

I stood and faced him across the wide room.

"You are dismissed, Becca," I said coolly.

Her sting of pain vibrated through the air, but I had to hide what was in my heart to keep Becca safe. As long as I did not make a fuss—as long as I obeyed—Lord Blacknall would banish her to Aubrey Hall as a relatively safe hostage. If Lord Blacknall chose instead to turn her out into the world, she would be beyond my help.

Becca curtsied stiffly and shuffled out of the room. It took all my self-control not to reach out for her. I turned from Lord Blacknall to check the arrangement of my hair in the small looking glass on my dressing table.

"That's the spirit, Katherine," Lord Blacknall said, leering into the mirror and preening his blond mustache. "We want you looking your best, and I have the perfect addition."

He produced a thin wooden box and opened it. Several gold hairpins topped with pearls winked in the candlelight. "A wedding gift."

"I have no need of them, sir." I finger-curled a disobedient blonde lock.

"Surely, you want your groom's affection, silly poppet."

An ally. If I could just have my husband as an ally, I would be satisfied.

"A few pearls will hardly make up for any deficiencies in my looks or my personality," I said.

"A little wealth goes a long way toward creating the illusion of beauty, and from thence follows love."

"Love is a form of madness. It does not afflict me."

Lord Blacknall chortled, a sound like a millstone crushing gravel. "That is why you have always been one of my favorite wards. Practical girls are so easy to deal with."

He drew out one of the golden pins and pushed it into my hair, scraping my scalp. I refused to cry out. I was *not* easy to deal with, but I would not show my pain. As he inserted the rest of the hairpins, I stared straight ahead, past our reflections in the mirror. He could decorate me like a marionette in a street show, but I was not accepting his gift. Not truly. With each prick against my scalp, I counted the value of the gold and pearls.

They would help me buy back control of Aubrey Hall and protect Becca and the others.

"You are not going to be difficult, are you?" He shoved in the last hairpin.

"Nay, sir, we have an agreement."

"Aye, your father's estates are safe. For now."

I nodded curtly. A heavy weight pressed on my stomach at his *for now*, much tighter than the boning in my stays. The woods and fields where my father had taught me to ride. The ancient halls where my few memories of my mother lingered. The tenants who depended on the lands for their livelihood. It all rested on me. I was placing my heart on the altar for them.

"Let us be off," Lord Blacknall said. "Your groom awaits."

I turned from the mirror and followed him across the bare wooden floor. I paused at the threshold to consider the chess set on the side table. The pieces stood in their lines, awaiting orders to go into battle. Making sure Lord Blacknall was not watching, I snatched the queen from the set, her stylized crown pressing into my palm. She was the most powerful piece, darting across the board, coming in unexpectedly for those who were not watchful. I tucked her into the pouch hidden in my skirts.

❧

Lord Blacknall's carriage jolted along the road despite the plodding pace of the horses. I had plenty of time to contemplate my future, locked alone in the bumping coach with the curtains closed to keep the dust off my silk dress. But I did not know what to dream of. I was marrying a stranger. I hoped that my groom—Thomas Westwood, that was his name—hated our guardian as much as I did. That he would help me regain

Aubrey Hall. His estate was called Wishwood. That at least sounded promising.

The carriage slowed even more, and I peeked out of the curtain. Weather-beaten stone cottages sat among patchy fields of barley and oats. A haze of smoke hung in the air, trickling up from several kilns where colliers made charcoal at the edge of the woods. Hired workmen trod through the trees, hacking away at the precious timber that should have belonged to the manor house and the village. It appeared that my future husband had not bargained well enough with Lord Blacknall to protect his own estates.

A loud thump drummed the side of the carriage. I peered out in time to see a youth with fair hair and a soot-stained face hurl another lump of mud at the carriage. A few other villagers had stopped to stare at my progress, their eyes cold and hard as iron.

Lord Blacknall brought his mount up beside the carriage and waved an arm at the villagers. "Vermin! Be off!"

When they did not disperse immediately, he charged through them, not even slowing for a young child who did not toddle out of the way.

"Look out!" I shouted.

The soot-stained youth snatched the child from in front of the horse's hooves. The other villagers sulked away like beaten dogs. I sat back and squeezed my eyes shut, imagining the tenants at Aubrey Hall subjected to the same cruelty.

We turned up a narrow path toward the house. Here, the woods were still thick, but I poked my head out to get a glimpse of my new home. The great stone ribs of a ruined church nave appeared over the trees, stretching out for each other like lovers trying to brush fingertips but crumbling apart before touching. Once, this had been a priory, but it had fallen to the greed and lust of King Henry VIII when he seized the church's lands and sold them off a century ago.

As we rolled closer, the priory house came into view. The square stone building, two stories high, sat in the shadow of the church ruins. A wall pierced by arches connected the main house with a smaller side building and stable. The carriage stopped. Lord Blacknall dismounted from his gray gelding and opened the carriage door for me. I stepped down and examined my new home.

Someone had a sense of humor to name this hulk of moldering stones Wishwood. Several of the windows bore jagged cracks, and they were all too dirty to allow me a glimpse inside. Several chimney stones tilted as though barely clinging to the rest of the building. Was it only Lord Blacknall who let the house become so neglected? My husband might help me take control of my estates after we were married, but it would do no good if he managed them no better than Lord Blacknall had.

Something moved in a broken window frame above. A pale, inhuman face stared at me, unblinking. A barn owl. I shivered at its knowing stare. What else might haunt such a ruin?

Lord Blacknall watched the owl, his eyes narrow and mocking. He glanced at me, his face full of some secret amusement.

"Is my husband-to-be a lunatic or imbecile?" I asked.

"Will you still marry him if he is?" Lord Blacknall asked, extending an arm for me.

I held my skirts and walked past him. "You have left me no choice."

Lord Blacknall followed me up the stone stairs. The edge of one step crumbled underfoot. I wondered if the house would hold up long enough for me to move in.

Lord Blacknall stepped forward and shoved open the worn oak door. The odor of dust and dank stones rolled over us. I wrinkled my nose and stepped through the shadowed doorway. A nearly empty great hall waited for us. The blackened fireplace had gone cold, and part of the railing was broken away from the stairs leading up to the gallery above. Only a few worn chairs sat near the hearth, their embroidered cushions flat and faded.

In an hour's time, I would be mistress of this dilapidated hall, with all its cobwebs and dirty rushes. Resident owls were the least of my problems.

"You don't belong here!" a scratchy voice called from the gloom.

I drew back, and a hunched-over person, perhaps as old as the priory house itself, materialized from the shadows and shuffled toward us like some decaying guardian spirit. I guessed it was a man because the creature wore pants. His watery eyes and wisps of white hair made a perfect match with the tired wooden chairs before the fireplace and the faded tapestries on the wall, all relics from a former century.

Lord Blacknall laughed. "But *here* belongs to me, Hughes. You would do well to remember that."

Hughes glared at both of us, trembling; whether from anger or age, I could not guess. The old man finally grunted and shuffled off to whatever dark corner he lurked in, and Lord Blacknall glanced back at me.

"Smile, my lady. We would not want dear Thomas to think you're unwilling."

I tightened my fist until my ring bit into my palm. "We have an agreement, sir. I will not back out of it."

"That's a good girl."

He patted my cheek, and I steeled myself to his touch. The scars on my back testified to the violence he inflicted when crossed, but I would not let him break me. I would turn this marriage against him.

Lord Blacknall led me through the hall. The dust motes drifting in the faint beams of sunlight swirled away from his path before settling back into their serene flight. I gently swished my hand through the ethereal glitter.

The doors at the far end of the great hall stood open, and I followed Lord Blacknall into the chapel. I entered the room as Katherine de Aubrey and would leave it as Katherine Westwood.

The chapel was dimmer than the great hall but smelled fresher. Someone had been burning rosemary for incense. Thomas Westwood was no Puritan, then, though he cared enough for religion to keep his private chapel in order. That, or he wanted it presentable for his wedding. A hopeful sign. I quickened my steps.

Three strangers stood at the front of Wishwood chapel before a wooden sculpture of Christ on the cross. One was clearly the vicar, with his white surplice and the Book of Common Prayer. The second was much too old to be a ward of Lord Blacknall, so he would be the second witness: one of Lord Blacknall's henchmen, no doubt. That left the third.

I squinted in the dim glow of the rushlights to study my groom. His long black hair and olive skin more Italian than English. Combined with a dark-colored doublet and breeches, it made him fade into the dusky background, especially compared to the fair-haired gaudiness of Lord Blacknall and his friend. I guessed my groom to be eighteen or nineteen, but it was hard to tell in the low light. His face was attractive, though rather stern. I tried to catch his eyes, but he stared straight ahead, seeming not to see anything.

I hesitated in my steps. Was Thomas Westwood an imbecile after all? The law would prevent him from marrying. If Lord Blacknall were honest. Which he was not.

I squared my shoulders and faced the vicar. I allowed one last glance at my soon-to-be husband. His eyes focused on me for a moment—clear and intelligent, with a hint of amused curiosity as his gaze caressed my face. Not an imbecile, then. I looked away quickly, my cheeks warm.

The vicar went through the motions of the ceremony. I responded where appropriate, hardly focusing on the words. I was much too aware of this stranger I was binding my life and my hopes to. Was it just my imagination, or was he stealing glances at me too? His jaw was strong and his deep brown eyes were bright in the rushlights. I assumed he did not want this marriage to a stranger either, yet I hoped he was not regretting it too much now.

The vicar's drone intruded on my thoughts. "Wilt thou obey him, and serve him, love, honor, and keep him, in sickness and in health; and, forsaking all other, keep thee only unto him, so long as ye both shall live?"

Could I promise to obey this stranger? To love him? My father had taught me not to take vows lightly. Yet I was doing this for my father's memory and for everyone at Aubrey Hall.

"I will," My words echoing off the stone walls of the little chapel. *I will, I will, I will.*

The vicar went on, "Who giveth this woman to be married to this man?"

"I do," Lord Blacknall said, a smirk in his voice.

I cast a hateful look at my guardian, and, in the corner of my eye, I saw Thomas's expression tighten. Thomas and I were pawns, moved across the board by Lord Blacknall's all-powerful hand.

At the vicar's urging, I recited my promise, "I, Katherine de Aubrey, take thee, Thomas Westwood, to my wedded husband, to have and to hold from this day forward, for better for worse, for richer for poorer, in sickness and in health, to love, cherish, and to obey, till death us do part, according to God's holy ordinance; and thereto I give thee my troth."

And now, I belonged to this stranger.

Thomas lifted a plain gold ring, and I extended my left hand to him. Father's *memento mori* ring sat on my fourth finger—the one whose vein led to my heart. Thomas's forehead wrinkled, but then he slipped his ring on to rest against the other and, prompted by the vicar, recited, "With this ring, I thee wed, with my body, I thee worship, and with all my worldly goods, I thee endow: In the name of the Father, and of the Son, and of the Holy Ghost. Amen."

He met my eyes as he said those words, and I felt a shiver of excitement and fear. There was something in his look—almost mocking, yet also intense and enticing. *With my body, I thee worship,* he had said. I would soon find out what lay behind that enigmatic gaze.

The vicar led us in prayer, and I blushed at my wandering thoughts. Yet this was my wedding day, and I was now a wife.

The prayer ended, and I stood still, my head down. My gaze wandered up to Thomas. He watched me uncertainly.

"What are you waiting for? Kiss her!" Lord Blacknall commanded with a chortle.

Thomas grimaced, and I stepped back. A poor start. But Thomas met my eyes again, and there was something in them, a mixture of defiance and humor. I smiled a little in return at the ridiculousness of the situation. He stepped closer and took my hand, his fingers strong and warm on my skin, and as sure as if he were going to pull me out to dance the pavane.

He brought his lips to mine, just brushing them, but it was like sipping hot spiced wine on a cold winter night. I parted my lips, and he kissed me again, lingering.

Thomas pulled away, and I opened my eyes to meet his expression of surprise and... concern? Before I deciphered his thoughts or mine, Lord Blacknall's voice broke the reverent quiet of the chapel.

"Excellent! Now, let's make certain this wedding is official, shall we? Take her upstairs, Gibbs."

Lord Blacknall's henchman grabbed my arms. Thomas tightened his grip on my hand, but Gibbs and Lord Blacknall pulled me away from him and toward the chapel doors. I struggled against their iron grips and cast around for help. I spotted one more witness to this strange wedding: a dark figure lurking on a bench in the shadowed corner of the chapel. The figure stood as though it might come to my aid, but then Lord Blacknall had me out of the chapel.

They hauled me up the wooden stairs. I tried to drag my feet, leverage myself from their hands, but my toes caught the edge of the wood and it splintered away. We passed through an upstairs gallery lit dimly by cheap rushlight torches. Then into a high-ceiling chamber with a bed, its curtains parted and waiting. They tossed me onto the straw-filled mattress and laughed.

My stomach lurched. Was Lord Blacknall expecting to turn my wedding night into a spectacle, too? King Charles had turned his nose up at that distasteful tradition, and I had hoped I might, too. I rolled and came up on my hands and knees on the mattress, fighting for some semblance of dignity.

"Now, we just need the happy groom," Lord Blacknall said.

"Gentlemen," said Thomas from behind them with a hint of sarcasm. "My health may be poor, but there are some things I can manage on my own."

The young man—my husband—stood firm by the door, arms crossed. His dark eyes belied his light tone, and his broad shoulders made Lord Blacknall and his henchman look small. Lord Blacknall stared him down, but Thomas did not budge. After several heartbeats, Lord Blacknall grunted and sauntered from the room, his companion in tow. Thomas shut the door firmly behind them and latched it closed.

I pulled my knees up to my chest, my hands trembling.

Thomas watched the door for a moment as if to make certain we were alone, then he turned back to me, his dark eyes impossible to read. His black hair fell in loose curls to his shoulders—a fashionable look, but one that seemed natural to him and not the result of vain preening.

"Well," he said.

"Well?" I responded, trying to not giggle with nervousness.

What did one say to one's new husband? I felt I should introduce myself, but he knew my name. He had kissed me.

He stepped closer, his eyes still on me. Then his gaze drifted away, and his mouth moved as though he were trying to work out something to say.

He scowled. "This is my chamber, but as I have just promised you all my worldly goods, I suppose I can allow you to sleep here tonight."

"My lord?" I asked.

"I am no one's lord."

He left through a side door presumably leading to a neighboring chamber. I found no voice to stop him. My fingers still trembled. The door closed between us, and I uncurled, fumbling for the comfort of a pillow.

Such was to be my wedding night. Humiliation, followed by... what? Sympathy? Or rejection? Why should it bother me? I had come looking for an ally against Lord Blacknall, not a romantic interlude.

I drew the bed curtains shut against the chills of the room and rolled over into the pillow to inhale deeply of the scent of sage and the piney spice of rosemary. A bundle of velvety leaves nestled under the pillow. Mugwort. It aided with sleep. Had Thomas not said his health was poor? Maybe that was why he turned from me. Why he would not even share a chamber with me.

Yet as I drifted off to sleep, I remembered that mugwort was also used to keep evil spirits at bay.

# Chapter Two

"Morning, m'lady!"

The bed curtains whisked back, and I groaned at the sun beaming down on me. A raven-haired girl about my age grinned and bobbed a curtsey before turning back to stoke the fire.

"Morning?" I mumbled, shielding my eyes with a pillow. Who was this overly cheerful female bustling about my room?

"You're right, m'lady. Morning's almost past, but I thought you'd be wanting something to eat, seeing as how you were traveling all day yesterday and getting married and all."

The young woman giggled. I shoved my face deeper into the pillow. I did not feel married, waking alone once again. But I was supposed to be mistress of this strange house that was far too bright in the mornings, or whatever time it was.

I pushed myself up, cringing at the light, and studied the bedchamber—my husband's bedchamber—more closely. It looked like it had once been part of one large room, but someone had divided it into two chambers, cutting apart the pattern of overlapping circles in the ceiling plaster. Other than the bed, there were a couple of chests, a chair, and a small table with a shaving basin and looking-glass. Two small doors led to closets on the far side of the room, and on the near side was the door leading to the other chamber. A tapestry of a man wrestling a giant serpent hung on the wall.

The young woman handed me a pewter plate containing a couple of overcooked eggs. I was eating alone, too, it seemed. The eggs were chewy, but I was hungry enough to eat them while the girl busied herself opening the window and airing out the bed curtains and linens.

"You'll be wanting your clothes and your own chamber, I'll wager," she said when I set the plate aside.

My chamber, where Thomas had gone to sleep. Was he still there? If so, it would create an awkward scene.

"Where is my... my husband?" I asked.

The young woman giggled, her black curls bouncing in the sunlight. "Up early this morning, m'lady. I suppose he did not want to disturb you. Oh!" She dropped a deep curtsey. "And I'm Sara, mistress. The master asked me to be your own maid now."

"Wonderful." I was to wake to this stream of chatter each morning. Did Thomas dislike me so much?

Sara seemed to guess my thoughts. "'Twas me or Margaret, and you would not want her. She's gloomy all the time. Can you imagine?" She grinned.

I wondered how offended the girl would be if I asked to trade.

"Very well. I'll need help dressing."

I stood, wondering if Sara would question why I was still in my wedding gown. She seemed blissfully ignorant, however, and followed me to the door connecting the chambers like a puppy promised a game of fetch. Lord Blacknall would not be so disinterested, and he would not be satisfied until he believed the marriage was legitimate.

I hesitated at the threshold of my new chamber, still afraid to find Thomas lingering there. Sara pushed the door open. A curtained bed took up much of the room, and a faded tapestry that depicted bounding deer covered one stern, whitewashed wall. The single window was propped open to the fresh breeze blowing in from the woods beyond the ruins.

I brushed past the bed and opened the door on the far side of the room. It led into a large closet filled with my trunks. The only other doors led to Thomas's room and the corridor. I peered out, but there were no other rooms nearby. Where was Sara to sleep? Becca had slept in my bed when I was a child, but I was a married woman now.

"Should we clear out this closet out so you have a place to stay?"

"I'll not be sleeping here, m'lady."

"Oh, you sleep downstairs?" That would give me an unusual amount of privacy.

"Nay, thank goodness!" Sara shivered. "I never stay in the house at night."

I stared at the girl. "Never? Why not?"

Sara smiled, though it looked a little forced this time. "I go home in the evenings. Oh, but I'll be sure you have everything you need before I go, mistress! I'll take good care of you."

"Very well." Maybe the girl cared for her mother or father at night? Certainly, she was not actually afraid to stay at Wishwood.

"Oh, these clothes!"

Sara rummaged through my trunks, lifting the gowns and holding them to herself to spin about. She was about the same height as me, if more buxom. We could make over my older bodices and skirts to replace her patched dress.

She sighed. "'Twill be like dressing a princess. But you're not a princess, are you? You're a baroness."

I smiled. "I will be a baroness when I can claim my father's lands and title."

"Who would have ever thought a baroness would come to Wishwood?" Sara worked on my lacings, slipping off my rumpled silk dress. "Of course, the Westwood men always marry... interesting."

"Interesting?" I selected a red bodice with puffed sleeves from my trunk. It set off my blonde hair better than Lord Blacknall's light blue silk. Not that it mattered what I looked like. Thomas had made his disinterest clear, and I was looking for an ally, not a romance. But I slipped on the red bodice for Sara to lace up.

"Course," Sara said as she worked on the lacings. "You must know that Master Thomas is half Italian. His father, the old Master Westwood, brought his lady home from his tour of the Continent. Cor! She was beautiful. Those eyes. 'Tis no wonder people said"—Sara cleared her throat and cinched my laces tight—"Well, sometimes, I thought she looked afraid."

"Of what?"

Sara pinched her lips together. "I don't know, mistress."

She was lying, but loyalty to her master's family was a virtue. "Can you tell me about the rest of the household?"

Sara hesitated and straightened my white collar. "There's Margaret like I said. Hughes does most of the rest of the work."

"That's a small household."

She shrugged one shoulder and helped me into my skirt. "'Tis just Master Thomas, and 'tis hard to find help out here."

"What about the village?"

She curled up her lip. "They don't have much to do with us, nor we with them. But they've had hard times ever since the old Master Westwood died."

That fit with what I had seen while passing through. A poor village would mean a poor estate, which would explain why Wishwood was crumbling. Good management would solve Wishwood's problems. Thomas had been ill, apparently, and was young to run a manor, but I had learned a great deal from my father. I would earn Thomas's alliance by helping him with his duties.

Sara arranged my hair, though she lacked Becca's gentle touch, and my eyes watered when she yanked at the comb. Out the window, I spotted a dark-haired figure moving through the maze of crumbling church arches. I needed to talk to my husband about Lord Blacknall, preferably without Sara. He had left me alone last night, but certainly, he would not ignore me outright.

"I would like to walk outside," I said when Sara released my hair.

"Course, m'lady."

She trotted along after me, but I would dismiss her when I met Thomas. We went down the stairs leading to the great hall and out the front door. I hurried past the ruins and into a garden behind the house, the boxwood hedges overgrown and the knots of herbs and flowers competing with weeds. Sara puffed for breath behind me. I kept catching glimpses of dark hair through the bushes or on the other side of a grove, but by the time we arrived, there was no one in sight.

"Where is he now?" I asked when we found the neglected rose garden empty.

"Who, m'lady?"

I gave her a sideways glance. "I thought I saw Thomas."

"Master Thomas never goes outside, on account of his health."

"Did you see anyone else out here?"

"No, mistress."

I frowned. I had seen someone. Maybe the other maid, Margaret. But it had looked like a man, and dark-haired, unlike Lord Blacknall and his henchman. The mysterious figure from the wedding? I twisted the rings on my finger.

As we walked the path back to the house, my boots smashed something soft: the heads of wilting roses. Someone had decapitated them and left the fragrant, shriveling petals spread over the path back to the house. I was certain they had not been there on our way out. I bent to scoop one off the ground, but the velvety petals fell apart at my touch.

After our walk, we stopped in the chapel for our morning devotions then ventured back into the great hall. After the cool green of the gardens and the rosemary scent of the chapel, the house smelled musty. Time to start acting like the mistress of Wishwood.

"We need fresh rushes," I told Sara.

"Aye, m'lady." She wrinkled her nose at the flat bundles of dried, decaying stalks insulating the floor and absorbing the muck tracked in by dirty boots.

"Long ones, if you can get them. I'll weave them into mats. They'll stay cleaner than these bundles." At least there were no dogs at Wishwood to soil them further. Thomas did not seem to welcome any kind of company.

Sara looked at me as though I had just proposed parting the Red Sea, but she nodded and hurried back outside. I would need a broom or pitchfork to clear the old rushes away and finding one would let me explore more of the house on my own. I began a search of the ground floor, starting with the great hall.

The image painted on the plaster above the fireplace was faded, but it had once been a lovely picture of a red stag. Beneath that layer, I could just make out an older painting, coated over by the stag. A round buckler shield and a pair of crossed rapiers also adorned the walls. Nasty things. Let them stay there where they would do no harm.

At the far end of the great hall, away from the chapel, an arched doorway led into some back rooms. As soon as my foot crossed the threshold, however, a figure appeared to challenge my passage: old Hughes.

The hunched-over steward glared up at me with brown eyes that had gone pale with age. "What do you require, my lady?" His tone did not match his polite words.

"I was hoping to find a broom to clear the old rushes."

"What would you be doing that for?"

"It needs doing. I have sent Sara to fetch some clean rushes."

"You sent that twit of a girl on an errand alone!"

I wanted to laugh at his alarm, but what if there was danger in the neighborhood that I had not considered? "Is it unsafe?"

He grumbled to himself. "'Tis improper. Just like a lady wanting to sweep. As if I cannot look after the place."

He retreated into the dimness, and I moved to follow, curious about the servants' domains.

A broom staff whisked close to my nose. "Now what?" Hughes waddled out of the darkness.

"I was just—" I glanced back down the dim corridor.

"Don't you bother with us." He grinned, revealing numerous missing teeth. "You have your own problems to deal with."

I did not want to be swatted with the broom like a naughty child, so I ceded the corridor to Hughes. He began a slow, methodical sweep on the far end of the great hall. It might take him all month to clean it out at that rate, but the way he glared at me with almost every sweep made it clear he would dismiss my help. I made a strategic withdrawal up the stairs.

That brought me to the gallery. I had seen little of it passing through to the bedrooms. It was a long, narrow room meant for walking in poor weather. A tapestry like the ones in the bedchambers hung in the corridor leading to those rooms, this one embroidered with a priest's walking stick sprouting into a tree.

Several generations of portraits watched me from the wall. The men shared light hair and a look that spoke of an adventurous spirit. The Westwoods bore no noble title: they had come by their high status through wits and work. And possibly through marriage. After all, the next Westwood heir would be the Baron de Aubrey. Assuming there was one.

I studied the women caught in the frames. The more antique of them were also fair and had shrewd appearances; good matches to the Westwood men. One with red hair sent a challenging look as if asking if I were up to the task of managing Wishwood. The most recent—she was clearly foreign, with her dark brown tresses, smooth, olive-toned skin, and those eyes. Large, almost black, and a little sad. Or, as Sara had suggested, trying to hide fear.

I had the sudden sense I was being watched and glanced over my shoulder, but no one was there. I rolled my shoulders and turned back to the paintings.

The last portrait hanging at the far end of the gallery had to be Thomas as a child. He favored his mother, with his olive complexion and rather distant, almost-black eyes. But something had interrupted the painter, and parts of the portrait were only vaguely sketched in.

A long wooden table was shoved to the side of the gallery. I ran my fingers through the slithery layer of dust on the table then brushed it off. Once, the household might have dined together at this table, but not recently. A couple of smaller tables sat at odd angles overlooking the hall below. On one sat a chessboard made of honey-colored oak and dark, polished walnut wood, with playing pieces of ivory and amber.

I paused at the table and traced the edges where the dark and light squares of the board met at perfect right angles. My father had played chess with me often, but Lord Blacknall used it to manipulate me, rewarding me when I played well and punishing me when I played poorly. I touched the ivory-colored pieces before me. They were so delicate that my breath could have knocked them over. I caressed the edges of the queen's crown.

She was powerless trapped behind the pawns. She needed to be free. I moved the king's pawn forward two squares, then stared at the red-brown pieces across from me. It was wrong to move them myself. I needed an opponent. Of course, I had Lord Blacknall for that. What I needed was an ally.

I ventured toward the door on the other side of the room. I pushed it open, but it slammed shut in my face. Were there defiant servants hiding in every corridor of Wishwood? I huffed and pushed the door again, leaning against it to hold it open. A cold wind pressed at the door and whipped me in the face.

What I had taken for a wall from the front of the building was actually the remnants of a bridge-like walkway connecting the main building, which had probably housed the head of the religious order, to a side one that I guessed had been the dormitory for the rest of the monks. The walkway itself was roofed, with a low stone wall on each side. Arched openings overlooked an overgrown cloister on one side and the woods on the other.

The stone walkway appeared solid enough, and the arches were weather beaten but mostly intact, so I edged out into the open-sided corridor. When I got over the rush of dizziness from seeing the ground far below, it was liberating, as if I were a squirrel running across a branch.

I hurried to the door on the other side. It swung inward. I stepped inside and shut the door behind me, leaning against it. Here was a corridor so normal-looking it was hard to believe that I had crossed the sky to reach it.

"Blacknall has gone," a voice said.

I gave a start and turned to find Thomas watching me. His dark eyes studied me in the faint light of the slit windows along the walls. I thought again of our kiss the day before and a warm shiver ran up my spine. But Thomas's face was impossible to read.

He held out a folded piece of paper. "I convinced him the marriage was legitimate and there was no need for him to linger, but he did leave you this."

I took it without opening it. "Thank you. I'm... relieved. That he's gone... He was not who I was looking for." Why was I prattling like a fool? I fought an impulse to reach out to Thomas; I did not dare give him the chance to evade my touch.

Thomas seemed not to hear me. "I always put Blacknall in these chambers when he comes. They're above the stables." His lips quirked, and he met my eyes. "A bit inconvenient, especially since the man is afraid of the open walkway. But what is one to do?"

I smiled. Good. My new husband was no friend of Lord Blacknall. I stepped closer. Thomas smelled pleasantly of sage. I wanted to be close enough to really see those almost-black eyes.

"I suppose it gives you some privacy," I said.

He did not respond—simply stared ahead for several long seconds. My forehead wrinkled. Had I said something wrong? Then he shook his head and blinked at me. "You should not be wandering across the walkway. It has an... unpleasant history."

"This is my home now. I'd like to know about it—even the unpleasant parts."

He hesitated a moment, then shook his head. "The farther you stay from curses, the safer you will be."

Was he teasing me? "I do not believe in curses."

"You will." Thomas opened the door and gestured for me to go through.

Confused, I stepped out onto the walkway, expecting him to accompany me. But he closed the door behind me, leaving me alone on the walkway with Lord Blacknall's letter. A flash of white made me glance up. The barn owl perched above me, watching with its black, unblinking eyes. I shivered and hurried back across the walkway to the gallery.

# Chapter Three

I stood in the gallery, Lord Blacknall's note clutched in my hand. Below, in the great hall, Sara had found a pitchfork to help Hughes with the rushes, but my mind was on husbands who believed in curses and maids who would not sleep in the house. I would have to clean the superstitions out of Wishwood along with the cobwebs and stale rushes.

Lord Blacknall probably knew of this supposed curse when he sent me here, though I doubted he believed or cared. I was tempted to toss his letter in the fireplace and watch it dissolve to ash, but I had to heed Lord Blacknall for the sake of Becca and everyone at Aubrey Hall. I broke the wax seal to read his scratchy handwriting.

*Lady Katherine,*

*I leave you now in the care of your new husband, but do not think you are forgotten. I will return when my business allows it, and until then, I have eyes around Wishwood who will tell me if you are troublesome.*

*Blacknall*

I crumpled the paper. It would go into the flames after all. Of course, his lordship would have spies. He would not allow me the sweet peace of being able to trust those around me. Of having anyone I could lean on when I grew weary of his games.

Sara had piled clean, dry rushes near the door. I walked downstairs and drew a chair over, trying to steal some light from the dusty windows. My fingers hardly needed it, though, as I plaited the rushes, making long, golden strips that I would bind together into rugs. The rushes brought with them the sweet scent of life, growth, and the outdoors, but it seemed such a small victory compared to the stubborn mustiness of the house.

Why did Thomas let Wishwood fall into such disrepair? He was not foolish, and I did not think he was lazy or careless. I needed to break through his reserve and make him my ally. When I tried to decide how, I was distracted by unbidden memories of his dark eyes, inscrutable but so quick to flash with humor. Several times I had to undo my plaiting and make it tighter.

That evening, I dined in the gallery alone with Sara on a simple meal of barley pudding, which lacked cinnamon, pepper, or anything more than a little salt. I would have to speak to the cook about her recipes. Or was the food bland because of Thomas's illness?

"Where does my husband usually take his supper?" I asked Sara.

She shrugged. "Most days, he's shut up in the library."

"Wishwood has a library?" I had seen no such thing in my cursory exploration.

She swallowed a mouthful of clumpy pudding. "One of the old monk cells with stacks of smelly old books. No one but Master Thomas is allowed in it."

"Hmm. And does he eat the same thing as the rest of the household?"

"I suppose so." She took another bite of the pudding and grimaced.

"Do *you* like the food here?"

She grinned ruefully. "Hard to complain about regular meals."

I smiled in return and stirred the muck with my spoon. "I've heard rumors about a curse at Wishwood."

"That's just silly talk! Wishwood's not cursed. This is a fine place."

"You've never thought about working somewhere else?"

"Oh, nay, mistress. I never could!" And she dove back into her pudding with renewed gusto, as if to prove it was better than we both knew it was.

When we were finished, Sara escorted me to my chamber and helped me undress. I slipped on my blue woolen night-gown. Gray rain drizzled down the windows.

"If that's all, my lady, I have to be going home," Sara said.

"In this? Stay here tonight."

Sara shook her head, backing toward the door. "Nay, I cannot."

She swished out into the corridor and shut the door behind her. I stared at the shut door and shook my head.

For tonight, my husband was the mystery I wanted to unravel, and he had to come back upstairs, eventually. I returned to the gallery to wait, taking a seat at the chessboard. The board was different now: the dark king's pawn sat facing mine. It was a King's Gambit. Interesting. I moved the next white pawn forward and studied the chessboard, trying to guess which moves my opponent might make next.

The rush torches in the wall sconces had burned low by the time Thomas trudged up the stairs, his eyes tired. I stood to greet him, and he raised an eyebrow.

"Did our beloved guardian have some message for me?" he asked.

"Lord Blacknall is a... a parasite. That is why I need your help."

Thomas looked curious, and he moved closer until I felt his warmth, smelled sage and rosemary. "How can I help you?" The soft, rich timbre of his words resonated in my chest. But I could not afford to be distracted.

"I—we—need to get my lands back from Lord Blacknall."

"I had the impression that that was why you agreed to this marriage."

I flushed, but I was glad he was being direct. "In part. Lord Blacknall agreed not to plunder my lands if I married, but I still need to sue out my livery."

"I know what some of those words mean, so perhaps that's a good start."

I frowned. He sounded too educated to be ignorant about political realities. "I have to buy my lands back from the king."

"I thought Lord Blacknall had them." His lips quirked in a faint smile. "How do your lands manage to get passed around like a bread bowl?"

"My father was a baron. He held his lands at the pleasure of the king. When he died, the lands returned to the king who rents them out to the highest bidder until I can buy the rights to them back."

"They sound like a great deal of trouble." He hesitated and studied me, his dark eyes guarded. "Were you planning on going back to live there?"

I stared off into the dimness of the great hall below, imagining Aubrey Hall lit by a hundred glowing candles, friends and neighbors gathered around the table for a feast at midsummer or Twelfth Night, the air ringing with songs and laughter. The world safe and ordered as it should be. "I... they are my family's legacy. There are people who rely on the estate for their livelihood—faithful servants, lifelong tenants. I do not wish to see their lands going to ruin."

"You mean like Wishwood?" he asked softly.

"Wishwood belongs to the king too."

"Does it? Strange that he does not take better care of it, then."

I could not decide if he was serious. "When you turn twenty-one, you'll have to sue out your livery to claim your properties. How can you not know?"

Thomas laughed, a deep, pleasant sound. "Lord Blacknall has been my guardian almost as long as I remember. He was selective about my education."

"I will teach you, then. Lord Blacknall can still control Wishwood until you're twenty-one, but I am seventeen—past the age of majority for females. That means if we sued out my livery, as my husband, you would have stewardship of my lands. A measure of freedom from Lord Blacknall."

Thomas's smile faded. "I am... not well, and I have little enough income as it is. I'm certain I don't have extra to sue out anyone's livery—yours or mine. I'm sorry I cannot help you."

He stepped away, leaving me cold. I gripped the double rings on my finger. "Then what am I to do?"

"You may do whatever pleases you, my lady," he said quietly.

He bowed and entered his chamber, shutting the door behind him.

I huffed and returned to my room, careful not to slam my door so he would not know how irritated I was. I should not have been surprised that he did not have extra income. Wishwood was a monument to decaying gentility. But there still had to be some way to redeem Aubrey Hall.

The rain continued its melancholy rhythm on my window, casting a haze over the ruins outside. I faced the cold bed. Before Wishwood, how long had it been since I'd slept in a room alone? Becca had shared my room as a child and later at Lord Blacknall's manor, except when I displeased him, which I often did, and then he took her away and kept a warty old woman to spy on me. When my father died, I'd stayed with my aunt's family, but even there I'd had a cousin to share my chamber.

That was where Lord Blacknall had found me. I had been so close to turning fourteen and being out of reach of the Court of Wards before he tracked me down. I had screamed for help, but my aunt and cousins watched helplessly as he dragged me away. After all, he had bought me from the king.

How often I had cried out in my heart for someone to rescue me. I implored God in prayer, wished on stars and Faerie circles, and begged with my eyes when anyone came to visit. But there was no one to hear. Heaven was silent, magic had gone out of the world, and everyone who saw me stared right past my misery. It was a desperate, falling feeling, to know that I was all alone and there was no one in this world who would ever take care of me again. So, I brushed myself off and decided to care for myself.

Outside, the soft hoot of the owl called to Wishwood. Nothing answered its lonely cry, and I wondered if it ever tired of sailing the silent night skies with nothing but ghosts and shadows as companions.

A sliver of moon broke through the storm clouds, and I peered out over the damp ruins of the old church below. A flash of white moved behind a decaying arch. A chill prickled down my back. I pressed my forehead against the cold glass, trying to see better.

Something white ghosted across my view. I muffled a scream. 'Twas only the barn owl, with its strange, almost-human face, gliding past the window. I stepped back, laughing at myself and clutching my trembling hands. I must not let my imagination get the better of me.

But there was an odd glow in the mists beneath my window, casting a warm orange circle brighter than the pale moonlight. A light, perhaps coming from downstairs.

I lit my tallow candle from the fireplace embers and eased the door open. The hinge wailed. No light showed beneath Thomas's door. I crept across the gallery. The rushlights were out, but the polished glow of the chessboard reflected my candle.

A rattle from the walkway door made my hairs stand on end. I crept over and laid my hand on the knob. Lord Blacknall was gone, so who would be sleeping in the far chambers? At night, such a walk would be dangerous, more so with the rain pouring down. I opened the door to peer out, and my candle's flame sputtered in the wind.

A figure in white stood on the far end of the walkway, hazy in the mist of rain. The figure seemed to glance back for a moment, then it vanished into the shadows.

I swung the door shut and backed away. What had I just seen? A ghost? Nay. That was nonsense. But someone was roaming the house. Perhaps Lord Blacknall's spy. This was my chance to flush him out. I headed for the stairs.

I crept across the great hall and into the dimness of the servants' realm. Three doors were firmly closed against the night, and the corridor opened into a kitchen. The fireplace was swept and banked for the night, so someone was caring for it. Perhaps gloomy Margaret.

"Good evening," a male voice said from the shadows. "And who is this pretty goose?"

I swung the candlestick at the figure lurking behind me. The slim man easily dodged the blow and responded with a mocking laugh.

"'Tis a bold thief we have here," he said, "assaulting the rightful tenant while you make off with the pewter."

"Thief?" I straightened and flicked back my hair. "I'm nothing of the sort. I am the mistress of Wishwood. Who are—"

"The mistress of Wishwood?" The man stepped close enough for me to see him clearly. He had dusty brown hair and a way of looking down his nose that raised my hackles. "So, Thomas finally conceded to the marriage, did he? I would say poor Thomas, but it looks like he fared far better than I expected." He gave me an appraising look that nearly earned him another swing of the candlestick.

"Who are you, then?" I demanded. He was dressed too well for a servant, and his lack of knowledge about the wedding meant he was not the person I had seen in the shadows of the chapel. His doublet and breeches were rain-splattered but red and blue instead of white, so he was also not the figure on the walkway.

"Beg your pardon, *Mistress.*" The man bowed, though he kept his eyes fixed on mine. "Sebastian Westwood. Dashing cousin of the unfortunate Thomas."

I saw the resemblance to the Wishwood men in his fair face and clever eyes, though his looked colder than those of the dead men in the portraits, lit by bitterness instead of ambition. "And why is Thomas unfortunate?"

"The curse, naturally."

"What is the curse?" Perhaps everyone in this household was mad.

Sebastian chuckled. "What an innocent you are. You'll learn all about it soon enough, I'll wager."

I would not beg this ruffian for information. "And what else do you have to do at this hour?" I thought of the figure on the walkway. "Are you entertaining company in my husband's home?"

"Saucy." He laughed. "No, for tonight I'm quite alone. Though, you ought not to wander the corridors after dark."

I thought of Sara fleeing Wishwood at night and Thomas's mother who had been frightened of something. But my only fear was of what Lord Blacknall might do to my people and my home.

"I will not be chased off by curses," I said.

"Brave, for now," Sebastian mocked. "But will Thomas not miss you?"

I narrowed my eyes. "I have my own business to be about. I suggest you leave me to it."

"Of course, Mistress of Wishwood."

Sebastian swept a mocking bow and opened the door leading outside, leaving me alone in the cold kitchen. I shifted from foot to foot, listening to the distant scrabble of mice, until boredom overwhelmed my stubbornness and I made my way back to the great hall.

A faint scent like burning hair tickled my nose. I dashed upstairs to see the orange glow of flames in the gallery.

# Chapter Four

"Fire!" I shouted.

The bottom of the tapestry smoldered, and flames licked up the image of the priest's staff transforming into a tree. I raced for the jug on my dressing table and tossed the water onto the smoking needlework. The lovely embroidered tree now stunk of smoke and wet wool.

My pulse slowed, and I clutched the painted water jug to my chest. What had happened? The rushlights were out, but they had been burning when I spoke to Thomas. The draft might have freed some loose embers to fly into the tapestry. But wool did not burn easily. Perhaps if it was mixed with linen.

Regardless, if I had not been awake, the fire would have spread and no one would have known. No one had come when I called. Were accidents like this why the residents of Wishwood believed in a curse? I shivered and hurried for my room.

I stirred the fireplace to be sure the coals were cool, then crawled into the bed. Under the chilly covers, I wished for

Becca, or Sara, or even my strange husband to reassure me that all would be normal again by daylight. Instead, I had only the quiet whispers of the night to keep me company as I drifted into dreams of smoke and ghosts.

Sara woke me again the next morning with her bright chatter and presented me with breakfast in a pewter bowl. Barley pudding. Leftover barley pudding. Now, it had cold lumps.

I was hungry enough to manage several mouthfuls, but I gagged on a thick, tasteless blob and set my spoon down. The food might be plain for Thomas, but it should be fresh. Lord Blacknall controlled everything about my life, but at least I could have a decent meal, even if I had to prepare it myself. I would take the matter up with the mysterious cook.

"There was a fire last night," I told Sara as I selected my dress for the day and stepped into the skirt.

"A fire? Here?" She paused from helping me with my bodice and looked around the room.

"The tapestry in the corridor."

"Oh. I wondered why it was dripping," she said with cheerful unconcern.

"Do things like that happen here often?"

She regarded me with wide-eyes. "Nay, mistress. There's never been a fire before."

"I suppose it was lucky it did not do more damage."

She nodded and drew the comb through my hair. "And what are we to do today?" she asked like a child anticipating the next game.

An apt question. I could not win my game unless I understood all the players.

"I met a person who claims to be my husband's cousin. Sebastian Westwood? Do you know him?"

Sara's expression darkened, and she bit her lip.

"You may speak freely to me," I urged.

She glanced around, like someone might be hiding behind the tapestry, then whispered, "I don't like him. The way he looks at me. It makes me feel like a rabbit in a poacher's snare."

"Is he here often?"

"He comes and goes as he pleases. I'm happier when he goes, and I don't ask any questions of him if I can help it."

I nodded. At least that verified he was real. And the figure on the walkway? "Does he stay in the other side of the building?"

"Aye, my lady. He and Master Thomas don't much care for each other."

I nodded. Sebastian was not the figure on the walkway, but maybe he lied about keeping company in the house.

"Does anyone else come and go from here?"

"Sometimes. Lord Blacknall or his guests might stop over. But I keep away from them if I can help it. They always stay in the other part of the house, and I don't have to go over there often."

"Hmm." So, there might have been someone else lurking about this place. "For today, I'd like to work on tidying up and have a talk with the cook."

"You're going down to the kitchen?" Sara asked.

"Is there a reason I should not?" I could not tell if she was surprised the lady of the house would visit the kitchens or if the area was usually off-limits.

Sara blinked like she had remembered whom she was talking to. "Course not, my lady."

We descended to the chapel to say morning prayers. The room was dusted, a contrast to the rest of the house, and the air still smelled of rosemary. It was not just for our wedding, then. This room warranted attention that the rest of the house did not receive.

After our devotions, I sent Sara to find some rags for dusting and marched off to enter the sanctum of the kitchen. As soon as I stepped through the arched entrance to the servants' area, Hughes materialized before me, like some cobweb-covered knight guarding a decrepit relic of the past.

"Good morrow, my lady," Hughes said, not at all friendly.

"Hughes." I nodded in acknowledgment. "I need to speak to the cook."

He glanced back over his shoulder. "That will not be possible. The kitchen is quite disordered right now. Not a fit place for a lady."

"Nonsense. 'Tis my duty to oversee the management of the house. If it is disordered, then it needs my attention."

Hughes glared, his age-paled eyes suddenly sharp. "*I* oversee the management of the house. Have been since the time of Master Thomas's grandfather."

I studied this odd specimen. Was it possible the former mistress of Wishwood had let Hughes have his way? Thomas's mother was foreign, so perhaps she had deferred to someone who knew the history of the place. Maybe she had not been allowed to do things her own way.

"I understand that things may have been that way in the past, but Wishwood has a mistress now, and I will not be deterred from my duties," I said firmly.

"Nor I from mine!" Hughes barked, spittle flying from his lips.

The door to my right swung open, and Thomas peered into the corridor. "What is all this racket?"

I curtseyed to my husband while Hughes bowed. Thomas looked taken aback by all this deference. He glanced between us then fixed his glare on Hughes. "What is the problem, Hughes?"

I bit the inside of my cheek, trying not to show my dismay that Thomas turned to Hughes instead of me.

Hughes puffed up, as much as his stooped posture allowed. "This lady wanted to disturb the kitchen."

"She wanted to disturb it?" Thomas's lips twitched, and he glanced at me with amusement. "Were you planning to throw pots and pans about? Lay your sewing out on the butcher block?"

I allowed myself a small smile. "Not at all, my lord. I only wanted to see about the variety in the meals."

"The variety?" Thomas's forehead wrinkled in confusion.

"The lack thereof."

"There's nothing wrong with the food served at Wishwood!" Hughes spat.

"Of course not," Thomas soothed. He gave me a thoughtful look, and I wished I knew him well enough to guess his thoughts. "Lady Katherine, would you step into my study so we can discuss this?"

He was giving too much power to Hughes, but he knew how to handle the old man. And I was intrigued to see his study: presumably the library where no one was allowed. He gestured me inside the little room and shut the door on Hughes.

The study was no larger than my bedchamber, with most of the floor space taken up by a small desk and carved chair, but shelves lined three of the walls and housed hundreds of books. I gaped.

"You're impressed?" Thomas asked, very close beside me.

I turned to find him studying me with those unreadable dark eyes. For a moment, I lost my voice under his intense gaze. "My... my father had a small library, but I've never seen so many books at once."

Thomas touched the open volume on his desk reverently. "It was the original priory library. It came to my family with the building. Many of the books would have been destroyed, but the reformers overlooked us, so now their secrets belong to Wishwood."

There was something almost hungry in his gaze as he studied the books, and I looked at them with renewed curiosity. I reached to touch one at the same time Thomas did, and our fingers brushed. A jolt raced up my arm, and I flushed.

Thomas quickly pulled his hand away. "What was it you wanted to say about the food?"

I drew my attention back to mundane matters. "'Tis rather bland. I'm not sure if you're able to eat more variety because of your... illness?"

Thomas swiveled to stare at the shelves of books. "I've tried any number of things for my affliction."

"If you told me—"

He faced me. "You are dissatisfied with the fare Wishwood offers?"

"Are you not? I had lumpy, leftover pudding for breakfast this morning."

He grimaced. "Aye, it was not very appetizing. I will talk to Hughes about improving the offerings."

There was a dismissive note in his voice, but I chose not to notice.

"When do you normally eat?"

"When I'm hungry." He sat again at his desk and picked up his book.

"Why not dine with me?"

"I do not need an audience to manage my meals."

I braced my hands on the desk, trying to capture his fading attention. "I miss conversation."

"I thought Sara was quite talkative. Have you frightened her into silence?"

"Of course not!"

"That's settled then." He returned to his book.

I gritted my teeth. Impossible man! This was no way to form an alliance. "Did you know about the fire in the corridor?"

That got him to look at me again. "Is that what happened to my mother's tapestry?"

"It was your mother's?"

"She was fond of it."

"The damage might not be too serious. But I do find the fire strange. Is Wishwood... haunted?" I asked, flushing a bit as I did. "Is that the curse?"

"Have you been seeing ghosts?" he asked with his quirky smile.

"I think I have."

He leaned back in his chair. "There's only one that I know of. A monk. He wanders the gardens. That's where the priory hospital used to be."

"Is he the only one?"

"One is not enough for you?" Thomas laughed dryly. "Most of the ruins here were once the church, and though I imagine the saints disliked Old King Henry smashing down their home, they have not returned to complain about it. At least not to me."

He shot me a challenging look. “If you are bored, you’re welcome to go looking for them.”

“Thank you. Perhaps I will. Even ghosts would be better company than always being alone.”

He made no reply, only stared off vacantly. I turned and headed out of the room. Of course, ghosts did not haunt Wishwood’s gardens, especially not while the sun shone and birds sang in the woods. But with everyone distracted by their work, I could escape the madness of Wishwood for a short time.

# Chapter Five

I rolled up the scorched tapestry, braced it on my shoulder, and lugged it down the stairs. My stubborn, difficult husband had some fondness for it, and I wanted to repair it—or at least air it out—while I enjoyed the freedom of the gardens.

Sara saw me and moved to drop her broom, but I motioned for her to stay behind. I needed to think. The tapestry stunk of stale smoke and something else. Still damp, it hung heavily on my shoulder and made me stagger through the ruins outside. I found the remnants of a stone wall and heaved the tapestry up to unfurl it.

Its odd scent wafted around me. Musty wool, but something more. I sniffed the bottom of the tapestry where flames had blackened the edges of the design.

Brandy.

The tapestry smelled of brandy, and a dark stain discolored the lower portion.

In my short time at Wishwood, I had never had anything more to drink than the weak cider that Sara brought with our meals. So, who had brandy to pour on a tapestry?

The "why" was even more disturbing. It would be an odd accident for someone to spill brandy on the tapestry at the same time an ember or spark happened to blow onto it. Nay, someone had lit the tapestry on purpose.

A stone scraped somewhere behind me, and I spun to look. Nothing moved in the ruins, but I had the sense that I was being watched. Lord Blacknall's spy might be about. Would Lord Blacknall want to burn down Wishwood, with Thomas and I inside? I could not see how it would benefit him. Sebastian was Thomas's cousin and looked old enough to inherit, so if Thomas died, Lord Blacknall would probably lose the estate.

Sebastian seemed like the type who might keep his own store of brandy, though, and he was wandering about just before the fire.

As was the figure on the walkway. Assuming it was no spirit, there had been someone else roaming Wishwood last night.

I scrubbed at the stained tapestry with a soft brush. The smoke and the brandy discolored the needlework, but I did not want to give up on it. Thomas said his mother had cared for it. At Aubrey Hall, I had a few things to remind me of my mother—her portrait, the soft scent of her gowns packed away in a trunk—but now I had nothing. I thought I remembered her sitting in the sunlight and embroidering, but perhaps it was only a dream. The longer I was away from Aubrey Hall, the more worn and faded every scrap of my mother became. I bit my bottom lip and scrubbed harder.

After nearly an hour, I sat back and wiped my forehead. I had done what I could. Now, I needed the sun to dry the tapestry and bleach out what remained of the stain. I rolled my shoulders. I could not shake the sense that someone lurked nearby. The woods beyond the ruins were still—unnaturally so.

I left the tapestry to dry and cut through the gardens toward the house. Instead of offering freedom, the boxwood hedges and carefully arranged paths of the garden twisted like a labyrinth. A trap. I walked faster. Sometimes, I thought I caught an echo to my steps—an extra footfall on the path, though no one was there.

Movement in the woods caught my eye. A brown-haired boy of about ten huddled in the branches of an old ash tree, so clearly trying not to be seen that he was obvious. A rabbit snare lay waiting on the ground. I slowed my pace. The young poacher looked too frightened of me to be any threat. In other circumstances, I would have warned him away from poaching, but he looked hungry, and he could help himself to Lord Blacknall's rabbits for all I cared.

Hoofbeats crunched over the path to the woods. The young poacher vanished higher up the tree like a squirrel, and I ducked behind the boxwood, peering between branches. Sebastian rode by, his expression calculating as he guided a chestnut horse into the trees. Now, where would he be going?

Once he had passed, I tried to follow his trail, but the path into the woods branched several times, and I did not want to get lost hunting for him. On horseback, he might reach his destination and return before I guessed which way he went.

I turned back, hesitating as I picked my way down deer paths toward Wishwood. The stone ribs of the church ruins reached above the trees and helped guide me.

The path ended in a grassy field dotted with stone and wooden markers. The graveyard. I hesitated then tiptoed inside. At least in daylight, I had no fear of meeting ghosts. The sleeping monks of the priory would certainly be proper spirits and keep their haunting to the nighttime. They also seemed unlikely to start fires or spy on one in the garden.

Many of the graves were marked by simple wooden slats, but a few bore the name Westwood. I found what had to be Thomas's father among them: Peter Westwood 1575-1619. The space beside him was empty, and I searched through all the stones but found none for Thomas's mother.

Odd.

If the fire had done its work, would there have been a marker here for me, next to one for Thomas? How little of the truth that chilly stone would tell. Lady Katherine Westwood, Baroness de Aubrey 1615-1632. I recognized none of myself in that imagined epitaph. Neither spinster nor wife. Neither commoner nor lady. Not at Wishwood.

The shadows grew longer, and I decided I did not want to be out in the graveyard after dark after all.

I cut back to the herb gardens in the old cloister. Chickens scratched around the hedges, but no rooster harassed me as I approached the flock. That would not do. The flock would only shrink without new chicks. And other than the chickens, there seemed little hope for meat unless we were to hunt. Or rather poach, for the game belonged to Lord Blacknall.

The tapestry would take some time to dry, and more work waited for me inside. If I returned through the kitchen, I might catch a word with the mysterious cook.

I came around the stables to find Thomas standing under the walkway by the kitchen door, his forehead creased with worry. My heart gave a jolt that sent a flutter through my chest. Silly, but of course, I was surprised to see him there when Sara said he did not leave the house.

"My lord!" I gave him a curtsey, and he watched me suspiciously.

"Have you taken a fancy to mucking out the stalls too?"

"Sir?" I glanced at the stables beneath the other end of the walkway.

"You've set my great hall into an uproar."

"It needed cleaning, and you said I might do as I pleased."

"Sara and Hughes are arguing over the rushes. They've nearly come to blows."

I huffed to cover a chuckle at the thought of the two squaring off with broom staffs. "That was not my intention."

He smiled. "I imagine not. It does disturb my work, though, so I'll thank you next time you want to cause a stir that you stay around to supervise it." His tone was scolding, but his dark eyes looked more amused than annoyed.

"I hunted for ghosts, as you suggested."

"Ah, and did you have any success?"

"Wrong time of day for it, I'm afraid."

"Just as well. What would you find to say to each other?" His face grew more serious. "Be careful where you walk. I cannot vouch for the behavior of our guardian's hired hands, and the villagers are upset with us over Blacknall enclosing the woods and stripping out the timber."

I thought of the hungry boy in the tree. "Is there nothing you—we—can do for them?"

His eyes hardened. "They would do best to leave this place. There is nothing *I* can do for them, and I doubt they would accept my help if I offered it. There is no love lost between the village and the manor house."

"Would you rather I did not venture out, then?" I asked quietly, not sure if I would obey.

He stepped closer, his face losing its hardness. “I do not wish to keep you prisoner.”

A scraping noise echoed above us. We both looked up. A stone from the walkway overhead plunged toward us. I froze, but Thomas threw his arms around me and swung me aside. The masonry hit the ground with an explosion of stone and dust. I, in my shock, was still staring up. A shadow moved against the deeper shadows above.

Tremors shuddered through my arms, and I dug my fingers into Thomas’s doublet to still them. The warm scent of sage filled my lungs with each breath until I relaxed into the protection of his arms. He made no move to push me away, and I listened to the quick rhythm of his heartbeat matching my own.

“Are you hurt?” he asked gently.

I met his gaze and shook my head. He stepped back, brushing himself off. A cloud of dust settled around us.

I looked at the cracked stone lying on the ground near our feet. “One of us could have been killed!”

Thomas nodded, his jaw tight.

“That walkway is too dangerous,” I said.

“You think this was an accident?” he asked. Had he also seen something move on the walkway?

“Nay, this was the work of a person.” My eyes narrowed. “Sebastian!” Was his horse in the stable? Even if not, he might have left it elsewhere to divert suspicion.

Thomas’s pale face darkened a shade. “Ah, you’ve met my cousin, then. He would be happy to see me out of the way so he can inherit Wishwood, but he knows that will happen soon enough as it is.”

I frowned, unconvinced of Sebastian's patience. Then I reached a hand for Thomas. "Regardless, you saved me, my lord. Thank you."

He stepped away from my outstretched fingers. "I told you, I am no one's lord. And curses are unforgiving. You would do best to stay clear of me, Lady Katherine."

Before I found a response, he strode back into the house. I watched him go, my hands still shaking with fear and with frustration, and resisted the urge to scream at his stubbornness. Or to call him back to comfort me.

But that was ridiculous. He did not want me at Wishwood. And he might not be the only one who felt that way. Thomas seemed to think that someone—or something—meant to do him harm, but that stone—and the fire—could as easily have killed me. Sara said events like the fire were not common at Wishwood. If this trouble had started when I arrived, the best way to end it would be to leave.

# Chapter Six

I woke the next morning to gray clouds gathering over Wishwood. Sara brought me oat porridge with a wilted sprig of parsley by way of adding variety.

When I had eaten as much as I could stomach and dressed for the day, I led Sara down to the chapel. I said my prayer and then sat with my head bowed, working over the problem of escape from Wishwood. I mentally counted the coins and jewelry I had brought with me. It was a start, but not enough to sue out my livery. I had to pay a third of the value of my lands. So much. I clutched my hands to my stomach. If I helped Thomas economize, perhaps he would let me keep the extra. He would not mind seeing me go home to Aubrey Hall.

I glanced at Sara, who moved her mouth as she read to herself from the Book of Common Prayer. "What are your wages here?"

She looked up vacantly. "Wages, my lady?"

"What are you paid for your work?"

"Oh, I'm not paid." She shut the book.

"You are not?"

"Not in money. I get my meals here at the house, and a place to stay for my... um, for my mother. At Christmas, Master Thomas gives us a little money as a gift, and that's how I shift for the rest of it."

She looked at me warily, like I might take away the little she had. More likely take away the living for her mother, or whomever she was protecting.

"Is anyone at Wishwood paid?" I asked.

"I don't think so, my lady."

The heavy dankness of the house settled coldly around me as the picture became more clear. "And who buys the food and other goods for the house?"

"No one buys them. When rent comes due at the end of the harvest, the villagers bring by their grains and cider and things, and we live off that. If there's any money, it goes to Lord Blacknall."

I leaned heavily against the hard, wooden back of the pew and squeezed my eyes shut. The cook's parsley had not been a snub, then—it was probably the best the garden had to offer this morning. Thomas had exaggerated when he said he had *little* income. Lord Blacknall held Wishwood—all of us—in chains.

And Lord Blacknall knew when he sent me here that Wishwood offered no hope for me to sue out my livery and save Aubrey Hall.

I left the chapel and hurried up to the gallery to look over the great hall and chapel below. My prison. Inescapable if I could not sue out my livery. In fact, I needed to make up for being another mouth to feed until I left. No one would go hungry because of me.

I turned to the line of Westwood progenitors in their frames, but they regarded me impassively. They had done their part and earned their rest. I had to work out my own salvation.

My chess opponent had taken the pawn I left as bait. Now, my king was exposed. I moved my king's knight forward to block my opponent.

Lord Blacknall bled Wishwood dry, but I had squeezed lemons before, and I knew that, even when you thought you had the juice, there was more hiding in the pulp.

I turned my gaze outside, trying to catch a glimpse of the sunlight breaking through the clouds and casting arched shadows in the ruins. Dust caked the windows, blurring the view.

"Sara!" I called.

"Here, mistress!" Sara trotted over from my chamber where she had been airing my bed.

Mistress. It was time for me to be mistress of something, if not my own fate. "Where's that other girl, Margaret?"

"She's out in the garden, m'lady."

"The garden can wait. I'm going to fetch her. I want you to start dusting those windows. Get the cobwebs out of them and use some vinegar to polish the glass. We'll let some light in."

"You want me to clean the windows?"

"That's what I said."

Sara stared at the windows then back at me. "Is someone coming to visit?"

"Perhaps another time. But we're going to clean up Wishwood, and we need to start somewhere."

Sara stared at the dust and cobwebs clinging to every surface of the windows and the out-of-reach corners of the great hall, her mouth agape.

I pressed on. "You said Wishwood is not cursed, correct?"

"Course there's no curse." She clenched her fists. "They just don't know Master Thomas."

She said this with such feeling that it gave me pause. Loyalty in servants was one thing, but infatuation was quite another.

"'Twill be harder for people to believe in curses if the rooms are clean and we let some more light in. I know it is daunting, but we'll take it one room at a time. Start with the great hall."

Sara nodded, and a smile crept onto her face as she picked up a rag and stared down the first dirty window. I marched off to fetch the wayward Margaret.

It did not take long to find the girl. Woman, really. She was older than I was, with a few silver hairs showing in the dark brown locks stuffed severely under her cap. She cut ferociously at the fading roses, pausing at times to dab at her eyes with a lace handkerchief. Had they sent the maid with a sensitivity to flowers out to tend the garden? Everything at Wishwood was upside down.

"Margaret?" I asked.

The woman gave a start and turned red-rimmed eyes to me. "Aye."

"I've not yet met you properly, Margaret. I'm Mistress Westwood."

Margaret wiped her nose on the delicate lace in her hand. The handkerchief was quite a luxury for someone who earned no wage. It must have been a gift from someone, and not just a poor, enamored villager.

She curtseyed deeply. "At your service, my lady."

"I'd like you to come inside and help Sara with the cleaning," I pressed.

"Of course, my lady. Whatever you wish." She spoke softly, but her bottom lip turned out in a stubborn pout.

"Is something the matter, Margaret?"

"Oh, no. The dust is so irritating, but of course, if you want me to clean it..." She regarded me with wide eyes and then held her handkerchief to her nose and said, "A-choo."

Not convincing, but, on the other hand, she was working for only bed and board. I raised an eyebrow.

She sniffed and added, "My master wants the garden cleaned up, and that does irritate my eyes, and then Cook wanted sage, but I'm happy to do everything everyone asks of me."

I compared the dozen or so spent roses Margaret had clipped to the hundreds waiting on the bushes. "Perhaps your eyes will appreciate the break from the garden. And once the house is cleaned, there will be less to irritate you there. I'll take the sage to the cook."

Margaret dabbed at her eyes again and meandered off toward the house. It must have been devilishly hard to get good help at Wishwood. But, of course, how many people would work for no wages? Only those with a loyalty to the family and no other options.

Which brought me to the cook. I gathered an armful of sage from the garden, doing a quick inventory of what it provided us, and headed for the kitchen.

I stopped short in the doorway. A hunched-over elderly person with wispy hair labored over a pot in the fireplace. The figure looked like Hughes clad in a worn-out bodice and skirt.

"Hughes?" I asked.

No response.

"Hughes!" I said more loudly.

The bent figure glanced up, dropped a quick curtsey, and spoke in a creaky voice. "Aye, I'm Hughes. You must be the new mistress."

Was Hughes wearing a dress, pretending to be the cook? Was everyone at Wishwood mad?

I handed over the bundle. "You wanted sage?"

The cook stared at the leaves with watery brown eyes. "Oh, you brought me sage. How did you know? That will do finely in the pottage."

"About the pottage..." I surveyed the kitchen. No bread baked in the fireplace, no meat hung from the rafters. This close to when the villagers would harvest their fields and pay the rent in foodstuffs, the only things to go in the pot were those scrounged from the gardens: some wilted turnips and pale carrots, from what I saw. But a few half-full barrels of grain stood on the far side of the room. "Do you ever make bread to go with it?"

"You said bread pudding, my lady? Tasty, but we'd need bread first, and my starter got moldy."

The she-Hughes returned to the pot as though that were the end of the idea.

Hughes might not have known how to make a yeast starter, but I did. I fetched a small bowl and put some wheat flour and warm water in it, stirring it into a paste. Then I left it to sit somewhere warm so the yeast could develop. I would need to tend to it several times a day, but it would be worth it for fresh bread. The grain supplies were worryingly low, but I would make the most of them.

With that done, I returned to the great hall to join the maids in their work. Cleaning Wishwood and having fresh bread would not actually save the estate money, but it would make the time more pleasant while I found ways to do so.

"What is all this?" Thomas asked from behind me as I wiped a window down. His voice had an edge I did not understand.

"Cleaning," I said mildly, turning to face him.

Sara and Margaret glanced at each other, then disappeared with their buckets.

"This is what you've been doing all morning?"

"I also made a yeast starter in the kitchen."

He rubbed his eyes. "Why?"

"Because it pleases me. You said I might do what pleased me." I scrubbed harder at the glass, but it only streaked the dirt.

"And why does it please you to make a yeast starter?"

"It pleases me to have fresh bread." I curled my nails into the cloth and scratched away the filth. "And it pleases me to manage Wishwood better and save money so I can sue out my livery, save Aubrey Hall, and redeem my father's title and honor."

Thomas squeezed his eyes shut. "Is it fitting for your father's title for you to work like a scullery maid?"

I wadded up the cloth. "I do not have my father's title. I do not have anything, because Lord Blacknall took it all from me, and you will not help me get it back!"

My words echoed off the stone walls. I swallowed and stepped back, my face prickling with embarrassment. It was not Thomas's fault. Lord Blacknall was our enemy.

For a moment, Thomas looked wounded, but then his expression became unreadable again. He stepped closer to me, forcing me to tilt my head up to meet his eyes.

"It is a sin, is it not, to make yourself appear to be something you are not?" Thomas took the rag from my hand, and his touch sent a ripple of warmth over my skin. "Why should Wishwood be polished? 'Tis a false image, and we don't deserve it."

"Deserve it!" Uneasiness over false images and being called 'lord.' Thomas was more of a Puritan than I had imagined. "'Tis no sin to take care of that which you have. God has given you a stewardship, and he will hold you accountable for it someday."

Thomas stepped back, and I missed the crackling heat of his nearness. "The theologists tell us it does not matter. God has already chosen who is damned and who is saved." His annoyance turned to resignation. "We may fight it, but we cannot change it."

"They also say, 'Help yourself, and God will help you, too.' Surely, you've read the parable of the talents? The Master expected his servants to work and multiply the coins he had given them, and he rewarded them for their efforts." I grabbed the rag, pulling him closer. "You control your own fate, Thomas Westwood."

He laughed bitterly. "That, I know to be false. And I do not wish to see you—or anyone—wear themselves out slaving over Wishwood."

"Then don't watch." I took my bucket and left to work on the outside of the windows. Already, more light poured in through the glass.

# Chapter Seven

I scrubbed the outside windows until my fingers ached, and still, there was more grime caked on the glass. I tossed the rag down. Cleaning helped Wishwood look more inviting, but it did not solve my problem of needing to escape.

I leaned against the sun-warmed stone of the house and stared out across the woods. It would be easy to get lost among the trees. What if I just walked away? Joined a band of tinkers and wandered about the countryside. No one would miss me. But Lord Blacknall would be sure that Aubrey Hall suffered. My eyes traced the plumes of smoke drifting above the trees. Had he left anything valuable behind as he stripped the wealth from Wishwood's lands? I needed to find out.

The sun had already begun its descent over the ruins of the priory, and mist clung to the moldering old stones. The mist swirled away as I walked through it. The stone ribs of the roofless church stretched up as if imploring the sun to wait a little longer in the sky.

The woods welcomed me with the musty green smell of moss. 'Twas a shame Lord Blacknall controlled the trees. With King Charles claiming ship money from the counties and building a royal fleet, the timber would bring good money to Wishwood.

Something stirred in the woods, and I spun to face it. A large creature moved in the trees. White flashed behind the curtains of green leaves. I backed up, stumbling over a dip in the path. The white form drifted through the trees, sending the branches rustling.

I drew a deep breath, my neck prickling. Did ghosts rustle when they moved, like a wind pushing waves through the mortal realm?

The white form emerged onto the path. A horse. Nay, *horse* was too mundane a word for this creature. It was not a riding hack, a draft horse, or even a prize stallion. I had never waxed sentimental over horses before, but this animal sent a shiver of awe through me. Its mane, though tangled, hung in a long, wavy curtain over muscled shoulders. This was a steed for a knight riding into battle. Certainly, it did not belong to this world. Its silver-white coat glistened in the afternoon light, and then it was gone again, stepping lightly into the woods on the other side of the path like a vision from the past.

I gasped belatedly. It had to be a spirit. But what did it mean? There was such power in each movement, I wanted to follow it, but it was unwise to wander off the path, and there were stories about faerie spirits that led travelers astray. I had not believed them until that moment.

I walked forward more cautiously, not certain now what each bend in the path would bring. As I neared the village, the sounds of men's voices and the thump of shovels against hard earth drowned the birdsong. I approached on tiptoe, glancing through the trees to see the men digging a ditch in the woods. Stacks of timber sat nearby, ready to be hauled to a mill, perhaps. The villagers might have foraging rights on the land, but certainly, they were not allowed to harvest the timber or throw up banks and ditches. These would be Lord Blacknall's men. People to be avoided.

When I turned to go, I found a fair-haired youth watching me from the shadows of the trees, his eyes narrow: the same soot-stained villager who had hurled mud at my carriage. His cold look sent a shiver through me.

I retreated toward the house, taking another deer path that cut through the woods. The men's voices faded, and I was alone again with a pretense of freedom. But the ditches that let me walk in such solitude also prevented the villagers from fattening their pigs on acorns or gathering firewood for the winter.

As I walked, I spotted a familiar figure in the trees. The squirrelly young poacher clung to a branch, staring at me with wide eyes. I stopped and smiled at him.

"You'll have better luck if you move your snares closer to the house."

He looked around as if making sure I was talking to him and not another lad in a tree. "To the witch's house, you mean?"

A witch's house, was it? "Are you afraid?"

He puffed out his chest. "Nah. 'Course not."

"After all," I added, "'tis not the wild animals that would be cursed, would it?"

"I don't know." He hopped down from his perch and moved closer, his wide eyes full of secrets. "There's some witches what can change form. What if I snared a witch on accident?"

"I suppose she'd change back before you had a chance to eat her."

The boy scratched his wild brown hair, considering that seriously. "But what if she put a curse on me?"

"That would be troublesome. But how do you know the witch still lives there?"

"Everyone says we have to stay away. They call it 'Witchwood.'" He regarded me curiously. "Have you been to the house?"

"I'm... I'm a prisoner of sorts at Witch—Wishwood."

His eyes widened. "Did the witch catch you, then?"

"Not a witch. A wicked man. Lord Blacknall."

The boy relaxed, quick to overlook the real threats made of flesh and blood. "Oh, him. My pa complains about him all the time. Tearing up the woods and kicking people off their lands." He studied me with an appraising eye. "And he keeps you prisoner? I suppose someone ought to rescue you."

I smiled. "I'm working on rescuing myself. But perhaps we can be allies. I will help you decide the best places for your snares, and you can tell me more about the village and the people in it."

He shrugged. My young hero obviously thought storming a crumbling ruin a much better adventure than gossiping about his neighbors. "Nothing exciting happens here. I've heard about a highwayman robbing carriages, but we've got nothing to steal in the village."

"A highwayman?"

He shrugged. "I've never seen him. I never see anything interesting. At first, I thought it was interesting when the men came to the woods, but all they do is cut down trees, and everyone says to stay away from the woods, 'specially at night."

"But you don't."

"We've got to eat something. I guess ghosts are less scary when you're hungry." He lowered his voice and confessed, "I never walk about at night, though."

But there was someone who did. "Do you know Sara?"

He tilted his head. "I know a little Sara who's three years old. And I think that's the name of Peter Atwood's mum."

"Ah, none of those are the Sara I know."

What if everyone at Wishwood *was* a ghost? I shivered. But I'd seen them eat, and they felt solid enough at my touch. I smiled again at my new friend. "My name is... Kate." A name no one had called me since Lord Blacknall took me away from Aubrey Hall. A name that went with having a place. Being liked and wanted.

"I'm Hal Smithson."

"'Tis a pleasure to make your acquaintance."

"Lady Katherine!"

I turned to see Sebastian striding toward me. Hal gasped and fled into the woods like a startled hare.

"What are you doing here?" I asked, squaring my shoulders against my husband's obnoxious cousin.

"Ha! She asks as though she had any right to wander about the woods." Sebastian glared to where Hal had gone. "Consorting with the villagers? That's not safe."

I rolled my eyes. "The master and mistress of the manor are supposed to know their tenants."

"Not at Wishwood. The villagers despise everyone at Wishwood."

"Because they don't know us."

Sebastian smirked. "And what happens to villagers who associate with witches?"

I pursed my lips and glared at him. "Why do they think there's a witch at Westwood? Only because they don't know the place."

"Silly goose. They know it too well."

I would not waste my time in a cryptic argument. Instead, I turned and marched back for the house. Apparently, I was too far into its snares to escape just yet.

The tall arch of the ruins rose above the trees, and I slowed. The sinking sun glowed red through the mists, like flames lighting the house. I shivered. I would be sure the fires were properly banked that night.

I hurried for the front doors. A shadow shifted on the edge of my vision. A tall, hooded figure stood near the house, watching me.

My muscles seized. "Who are you?" I demanded, my voice trembling only a little.

The figure took a step toward me, revealing black hair and a dark face scarred by some long-ago brawls.

"I demand you answer me!" I cried, hoping someone in the house heard me. For one irrational moment, I wanted to cry that the windows were cleaner now—everyone should be able to see.

The man only turned and walked back into the ruins.

I took, long, trembling breaths. Spirit horses were one thing. Had I just seen the ghost of the monk? But, nay, this man had been dressed in modern fashion, not like any ghostly monk. The highwayman, then?

Sara hurried out to meet me, glancing to where the figure had disappeared. "Are you all right, mistress?"

"You saw him too," I demanded of Sara.

"Course I did. Master Thomas's uncle terrifies me."

"*That* was Thomas's uncle?"

"Master Thomas's mother brought him with her from Italy when she married the old master. He's odd, but he don't do anyone no harm."

I almost pointed out that Sara had just said that he did, in fact, do harm, but decided it was not the time for grammar lessons. "And where does this famous uncle stay?"

"Over in the other part of the house, when he's around. You'll see little of him. He likes to roam about the countryside. Don't want to be cooped up, I suppose, a bit like an old tomcat."

"Ah." So, he might have been the figure on the walkway. And the mysterious guest at the wedding. Could he also be the one setting fires and tumbling down stones? Spying for Lord Blacknall? The evening gloom fell quickly over Wishwood, casting everything into shadow.

"You should not go out there tonight, Sara."

"I must," Sara said quietly.

I sighed. "Can you help me change first? I'll meet you in my chambers."

Sara ducked in a curtsey and left to put her broom away.

"'Tis Spain, not Italy," a voice said from the doorway.

I gave a start and turned to face Thomas, who was leaning against the wall.

"Pardon?" I asked.

"My mother—and by extension, my uncle—are of Spanish extraction. My father met them in the Netherlands." He smiled. "I only thought I would clarify because if you accused Uncle Ignacio of being Italian, you would hear a string of words that are not fit for any lady's ears, even if they are in Spanish, and I would hate for you to scream at him again."

He turned to go back inside.

I called after him, "I saw a ghost on the road."

"Oh?" Thomas turned back at that. "Our monk does not usually wander that far."

"'Twas not a monk. 'Twas a great, white stallion, like a knight's charger."

Thomas's eyes grew distant. "Really? I did not suspect that fellow was still around. You might find he's more flesh than spirit, though as hard to catch as a ghost." He met my gaze with a challenging look. "If you can lure him in, you can have him."

"And he will not drag me off into some lake to drown me like a fairy steed?"

"No lakes around here for miles. You'll be safe." Thomas took a step toward me but stopped himself short. "I hope you stay that way."

He turned and went inside, leaving me chilled and confused.

I did not see Thomas again that night, though I heard him moving on the other side of the connecting door after Sara left me. At one point, I tip-toed over and placed my hand on the door. At times, he seemed humorous and understanding, and I thought I might win him to my side, but then the doors between us shut again.

The small noises of him readying himself for bed ceased for a moment, and I imagined him standing there, perhaps looking toward the door and thinking of me. Why did he keep me at arm's length? And why did I care? I could open the door, reach out to him, but my pride objected to the thought of being rejected again.

After a long moment, his bed creaked as he settled down for the night. I walked softly back to my bed and was about to lie down when I remembered the starter. If I did not feed it, it would turn into muck and I would never have my bread.

I groaned and grabbed a dressing gown then slipped out into the darkness of the corridor. The boards squeaked under my feet, so I pressed against the wall, feeling my way to the stairs. The scent of incense tickled my nose.

Half-heard whispers rode on the drafts. Someone else in the house was stirring. The sounds came from the chapel. Its heavy wooden door was shut tight, but a faint sliver of light fanned out beneath it. I stepped closer. Something rustled behind the chapel door. Was someone hiding just on the other side, listening as I listened? Mustering my courage, I leaned an ear forward, not quite pressing it against the wooden door, for fear the listener on the other side would sense the small disturbance.

Low voices murmured in the darkness, but nothing clear. It almost could have been the wind, except for the faint light and a certain rhythm to the sounds that suggested conversation.

A clank sounded from the gallery at the top of the stairs. Someone else was wandering the house. I slid away from the light trickling under the door and outlining me to anyone watching from above.

The sounds from the chapel cut off. I held my breath, caught between two unseen opponents. Whoever was in the gallery might just be one person, but I could only guess what kind of wickedness might be going on behind the chapel doors. A witches sabbath, perhaps? Was that why Sara would not stay here at night?

There was no other sound from the gallery. After a few moments, the murmuring sounds from the chapel picked up again. Witches, ghosts, what else haunted Wishwood?

I tiptoed back to the staircase and felt my way up. When I was almost to the top, something caught my foot and sent me sprawling forward against the hard stairs. I gasped then covered my mouth with my scraped hands. The chapel door stayed shut.

I fumbled around for what had caught my foot. A long, thin twine stretched across the second-to-top stair. It had not been there on my way down. If it had...

The draft shivered over my icy skin. If I had tripped over that twine going down, I would have done more than skinned my palms.

My hands shook. I ripped away the twine, breaking it where it had been tied to the banister. This was no accident. And it was no ghost. Someone of flesh and blood had been here, just a few moments before, intent on killing me. It could be anyone at Wishwood. Except for whomever was down in that room.

I clutched the twine and scurried for my room, bolting the door behind me. I needed to leave Wishwood, to flee to a haven of safety and sanity. I glanced down at the twine and to Thomas's door. If my husband wanted me dead, there were easier ways for him to be about it. And if it was Lord Blacknall's spy who wanted me gone, or someone else in the house, I would not let them drive me away. I would be happy to leave, but I was trapped. What did they want of me? Well, they would not win. Let them see me survive their snares. I would be on my guard the next time, and I would flush out this schemer and triumph over him. Wishwood would not be my undoing.

# Chapter Eight

I rose early after a restless night and tugged a nightgown over my smock to go downstairs. I might have to begin my starter anew, but we would have bread at Wishwood.

I stopped short at the end of the corridor. Thomas knelt on the floor, all the portraits from the gallery wall spread around him. A deep sadness creased his forehead as he gently smoothed back a tear in one of the canvases. I did not need to ask which one. His face echoed my pain when I thought about my mother.

Thomas glanced over at me and straightened, all sadness hidden and a dangerous anger glittering in his dark eyes. I took a step back then realized the anger was not directed at me.

"What happened here?" I asked quietly.

He gave me a tight smile. "The curse, of course." He cast a regretful glance at the portrait of his mother. A long slash cut through the bottom of the picture, but her face was undamaged.

"Do you know when?" I asked.

He shook his head.

"Last night, I thought I heard noises downstairs. After I checked on them, I found a string pulled taut across the stairs. A trap."

Thomas strode over to the examine the staircase. I pointed to where I had broken the string, but all traces of it were gone. Thomas frowned.

"I still have the twine in my chamber," I said.

He shook his head. "No need to retrieve it. Obviously, something occurred here last night."

"You don't know what?"

"If I did, I certainly would not have allowed this to happen." He gestured at the portraits.

"Someone is trying to harm one of us."

He stared back at the pictures. "Someone—or something—is angry." He turned back to me. "Watch yourself, Lady Katherine."

Then he whisked off down the stairs.

"'Tis Kate!" I called after him.

He gave no sign that he heard.

I lowered myself next to the picture of his mother, gently lifting the damaged canvas. I might be able to repair it. Next to it was the unfinished picture of Thomas. It had been slashed several times, far beyond my ability to mend. A sick feeling turned in my stomach. I carefully rehung each picture except the one of Thomas. That one I took to my room to ponder over then went back to the gallery to find breakfast waiting.

Margaret joined Sara and me, and we ate in silence. Sara happily worked on the poached eggs. Margaret studied the slashed picture with a frown creasing her lips. As she picked at her eggs, she mindlessly stroked the corner of her fine lace handkerchief.

When we had eaten all we could, I said, "We have more work to do today."

Sara looked all hopeful anticipation. Margaret glowered and studied her fingernails as if anticipating that I was going to ask her to sully them.

"You've done excellent work on the lower floor," I told them. Sara beamed, and Margaret smirked. I was not exaggerating. The great hall now had a freshly woven rush rug, and sunlight poured through the windows, except the broken ones we had covered over with cloth. "I want to work on the gallery next. The pictures... fell down last night. I have rehung them, but I want to clean the room. We'll polish the tables and dust the pictures."

Margaret dabbed at her eyes with her handkerchief, though they showed no signs of irritation. I was tempted to make her dust just for the subtle manipulation, but Sara did not care which job she did.

"Sara, grab a dust cloth, please. Margaret, some oil for the tables."

Margaret tried to suppress a triumphant smile, and I tried to ignore it. I fetched a needle to repair the worn seat cushions. I would need glue for the torn portrait, but I could fix that too.

As I sat sewing, Sara dusted in time to a country dance she hummed to herself. I looked about for my scissors, but I had forgotten to bring mine out of my trunk.

"What do you need, my lady?" Sara asked.

"Scissors."

"Use mine. They're fit for a fine lady—a gift from the last mistress of Wishwood when I was just learning to sew."

She left her work and hurried off. Margaret cast her a resentful look and polished on half-heartedly. She wore her fine handkerchief tucked into her bodice. 'Twas Flanders lace, possibly, from the Low Countries. Another gift from the former mistress of Wishwood?

Sara returned with a basket, but her smile faded as she rummaged through it. "I thought I left them in here, but I suppose not." She shrugged, unconcerned, and picked up her dust rag again.

Margaret rolled her eyes. The first table now shone as it likely had not had since it was new. She started to move the chessboard to polish the second table.

"Stop!" I tossed aside my embroidery and lifted the board for her to work under.

She looked at me as if I had lost my mind, but I did not want to interrupt my chess game. My opponent had moved another piece, and I now had the advantage.

As I returned to mending the frayed cushions, I thought what a shame it was that the household did not usually eat together in the gallery, especially now with the windows illuminating the room.

"Sara, when does my husband take his breakfast?"

Sara wrinkled her forehead and exchanged a nervous glance with Margaret, who looked at me suspiciously.

"It can hardly be a secret when he eats," I pressed.

"He breaks his fast early," Sara said. "He's always awake and in his study before I arrive."

I glanced at Margaret, but she just shrugged stupidly.

When Sara finished freeing the old inhabitants of Wishwood from their layers of dust, I had her help me unroll the clean and dry tapestry and hang it back on the wall. The edges were still singed, but a little stitching would keep it from unraveling.

"I'm glad this one is back," Sara said. "'Tis one of my favorite stories."

"Stories?" I asked.

"You know, of St. Patrick. He stopped to teach the people, and he was at it for so long, his staff rooted and became a tree."

"I had not heard that."

"The vicar used to tell it. He said everything is in God's hands. We just have to be patient." She smiled dreamily.

I caught Margaret rolling her eyes and resisted the urge to laugh along with her. "Trust in God is commendable, but I prefer to stay busy while awaiting his timing." I stared out the windows at the ruins beyond. "Sara, do you ever see anything odd outside at night?"

Margaret paused in her polishing for a moment but returned to wiping her cloth in lazy circles.

"Oh, you mean the ghost!" Sara said. "Sometimes there are odd lights moving about at night. I don't *know* if it is our ghost, but 'tis fun to scare myself by imagining it is."

"I've seen odd lights at night too, out my window."

"You saw him!" Sara clapped her hands and grinned.

Margaret made a disgusted noise and shook her head. "All this talk of ghosts is silly. 'Tis just glow-worms or some such."

I tended to agree there were no ghosts. The spirits of the monks might miss religious services, but ghosts did not go into chapels at night and burn rushlights. Neither did glow-worms.

Regardless of Wishwood's spectral residents, I needed to deal with the flesh-and-bone ones. Sara's story of St. Patrick had given me an idea. Thomas might not want to listen, but there was danger for everyone at Wishwood. I would not let him ignore me.

Fresh bread would have been better for my strategy, but my starter was not ready. Porridge would have to do. Rising with the predawn light the next morning, I dragged the small table and chairs from the great hall to block Thomas's study door. Then I waited.

He came staggering down the stairs not long after me, his black hair mussy and his eyes still tired. He paused when he saw me sitting there, then looked over his shoulder as though wondering if he had wandered into the wrong corridor.

"Good morrow," I said.

"What is this?"

"A table set for breakfast. Porridge, I expect. 'Tis not the most satisfying meal to me, but apparently you are content with it."

He gave me a withering look. "I'll take mine alone, thank you. Go find something more enjoyable to do."

"This is what pleases me."

"You're blocking the door to my study."

I smiled sweetly at him.

He rolled his eyes and slumped down in his seat.

"Hughes! Bring breakfast for both of us!" Thomas called, giving me a sardonic look.

The old steward appeared, casting me a look that would have curdled sweet cream, and delivered two bowls of porridge. He bowed to Thomas and departed.

Thomas picked up his spoon and ate in silence. I did the same. It was a small victory, at least.

Thomas rang a bell, and Hughes appeared from somewhere in the belly of the old house. "Send more cider, please."

"You'll be wanting your drink, young Master," croaked an ancient voice.

I gave a start. There was the Hughes from the kitchen, toddling up with a mug of cider for Thomas.

"That will do, Hughes, Mistress Hughes," Thomas said.

The matched pair bobbed their heads and hobbled off in separate directions. I stared back and forth between them.

"Well, what is the matter?" Thomas asked, looking honestly perplexed.

"There *are* two of them!"

"Two of... Do you mean the Hugheses? Did you think..." He watched my face flush red and burst into laughter.

I buried my face in my hands and chuckled along with him. "They do look tremendously alike."

"I suppose they must after being married for so long," Thomas said, failing to hide his lingering grin.

I smiled down at my porridge. "'Tis rather sweet to see a couple so devoted to each other that they become similar. I imagine my parents would have been that way if they had lived. And I..."

I flushed and looked up at Thomas, whose expression had turned serious again. I had always hoped for an affectionate marriage. Did Thomas not want the same?

We continued to eat in silence for a few minutes, but the strain was back between us, as solid as a locked door.

Thomas flung his spoon on the floor. The clatter made me drop my spoon, and I gave Thomas a questioning look. He stood quickly, catching his balance on the chair. "I am finished."

He dragged the table aside, barged his way into his study, and shut the door. I sat staring at the discarded spoon. Incomprehensible. Had I done something to anger him? 'Twas not a promising fresh start.

I rang for Hughes to clear away breakfast—Master Hughes, that was—and wandered back upstairs. The chess game sat untouched, but Sebastian was there, studying it with a frown. I gritted my teeth. I ought to have the self-control to avoid touching the pieces, but each new parry surprised and challenged me.

Sebastian made no move to touch the pieces, though, or to reference the game. Instead, he leaned back and propped his feet up on the table, scuffing Margaret's polishing and tipping over my bishop.

I righted the piece. "You certainly make yourself at home here. Do you not have somewhere else to be?"

"No place suits me so well as Wishwood."

"You enjoy playing the part of an uninvited guest."

"The saucy wench forgets to whom she is speaking. When my cousin succumbs to his afflictions, Wishwood may well be mine. I am over twenty-one. Lord Blacknall will not be able to control it anymore." Sebastian leered at me. "Provided, of course, that Thomas has not produced an heir. And how is that progressing, by the by?"

I ignored the bait. "*If* Thomas dies young, you will have to contend with his widow."

Sebastian made a shooing motion. "We can work out some arrangement. You wish to return to your father's estates? I can help you sue out your livery. And I will manage Wishwood better than Thomas or his lordship ever did. We'll all have what's best."

"Except for Thomas," I said.

"Who says the peace of the grave will not suit him best?"

"You're a devil!"

"I'm a realist." Sebastian rose. "He's a tortured creature. Leave him be. There are other ways to gain your independence. As a widow—"

"I will not listen to this wicked talk!"

"You will eventually."

"You're so certain he's going to die. Maybe you plan to do him harm."

Sebastian smirked. "Nonsense. For now, I appreciate your help in getting Wishwood cleaned up. Focus on that and don't worry about providing an heir. Thomas already has one in me."

I dearly wished for something to hit Sebastian with, but he judged his timing wisely and strolled away before I noticed the broom abandoned in the corner.

Sebastian stood to lose a great deal if I did produce an heir for Wishwood. And if I died in some accident? The spouse was the first one suspected in such cases. If it looked like Thomas killed me, it might clear the way for Sebastian to inherit sooner. Thomas had spoken the truth. I needed to watch myself.

# Chapter Nine

The next morning, I once again arranged a table and chairs in front of Thomas's study before daybreak. I was not ready to quit, nor to let Lord Blacknall or Sebastian win. I needed to gather my resources. I needed an ally—to not be alone.

Thomas came down, yawning, not long after I had settled myself at the table. He stopped short at the sight of me in his way and looked me over. I had arranged my hair to curl around my face and wore a red gown that flattered my figure.

"Good morrow." I gave him my sweetest smile.

"You're sitting in front of my door. Again."

"I thought we might break our fasts together each day. Come to know one another better. I'm not going anywhere, after all."

He sighed. "Do you mean that literally or figuratively?"

"Both."

He leaned close, so his face was even with mine. His jaw, set firmly, had just the faintest trace of stubble. I was sorely tempted to brush my finger over it, to feel its prickly tickle against my skin. Thomas watched me intently.

"I could move you," he whispered. "Lift you with one arm and toss you over my shoulder."

That suddenly did not sound like a bad thing—to be held in his arms. To inhale more of his sagey scent.

"I might struggle," I said, a little breathlessly. "Rouse the house."

Thomas's gaze lingered on mine, then traced its way down to my mouth. I leaned closer.

He looked away abruptly. I caught my breath, surprised by the stab of pain in my chest.

"I suppose I cannot have you making a fuss," he said. "If I eat with you, you will let me go back to my books?"

His books? I wanted to throw his precious books on the floor. To run back to my room and bolt my door against the humiliation of seeing him turn away from me again. But my father had taught me to stay the course. If I could press on after Father threw away his life, his duty, and me, I could also persist in the face of this. I needed Thomas to listen to me, not to love me.

I nodded. "I will."

"Very well."

He sat and rang for Hughes, and we ate our porridge in strained silence. Thomas finished first and waited quietly while I scooped out the last bites of sticky, tasteless oats. Then he rose, bowed to me, and pulled the table aside to enter his study.

Hughes came to take the bowls away, giving me a smug look as I sat there alone. If it had been in my power, I would have dismissed him on the spot, but it was not. Everything was out of my control.

Nay, not everything. I would find out who at Wishwood meant Thomas or me harm. I watched Hughes suspiciously as he tottered off with the dirty dishes. He did not hide his dislike of me. He was capable of setting a fire and tying a line across the stairs, but could he push over a large stone? And would he run the risk of hurting Thomas?

Sebastian was still my most likely suspect. I needed to find out how he spent his days. He had a horse, so the easiest thing to do would be watching the stables.

*Easy*, it turned out, but neither simple nor interesting. I made an excuse to Sara about working in the gardens and found a place near the house to hide in the trees and watch the stable doors. For the long wait, I brought a needle and one of Thomas's shirts, which Margaret had brought back from washing to show me a gash down the front. Whatever Thomas had done to it, I could not imagine, but at least I could mend it.

The sun made its slow way across the sky, shifting the tree's cool shadows and allowing strips of warm light to reach my hiding spot. The stump I had found to sit on soon grew too hard, but I forced myself to stay. The scent of Thomas's shirt made me feel like he was there with me, less lonely. If only he would stop turning away from me. We could be allies. Perhaps more.

I swallowed around the lump knotting in my throat. I was used to being alone. Why would that ever change?

The shadows were short and the sun high overhead when someone finally stirred around the stable. A cloaked figure slipped out of the door on foot and hurried around the side of the house. I scrambled to follow, trying to stay out of sight while not losing the trail.

As I reached the far side of the stable, hoofbeats echoed behind me. I turned in time to see Sebastian trotting off down the lane on his chestnut.

I stared back at where the cloaked figure had gone. Did Sebastian have an accomplice? Thomas's mysterious uncle, perhaps? I peered around the corner, but I had lost my quarry.

I hurried down the lane, listening for the sound of hoofbeats. A nicker echoed from beyond the ruins. I cut through the crumbling stones rendered bright and harmless by the midday sun.

A white form appeared from the woods: my ghost horse. We stood staring at each other for a moment. Had Thomas not said I could have the creature if I caught it? It would be easier to keep up with Sebastian if I had a mount of my own.

I whistled, and the horse flicked its ears forward. Slowly, so as not to startle the magnificent beast, I edged my way over to the garden and pulled a carrot from the ground. I whistled again and held out the carrot.

The horse took a few careful steps forward. I held the carrot out, my palm flat, not moving. One breath at a time, the horse crept nearer. Its velvety lips lifted the carrot from my hand. I lowered my arm and stepped closer. The horse twisted its ears back but did not flinch away from me. I ran my hands over its long mane and down its warm neck.

"So, 'tis true. You're no ghost after all," I said, inhaling the warm scent of horse and forest from the creature's silvery-white coat. "A gelding, I see. What a pity. You might have sired some lovely foals. But it must be lonely living in the forest, and soon people will come to cut down these trees."

As I spoke, I untangled the gelding's mane and scratched around his ears. He took the attention in stride, nuzzling around for another carrot.

"Quite tame, and not so young. If I found a saddle, you might make an excellent mount for a lady."

I hurried over to the stables. The gelding hesitated, then trotted along behind me. I peered into an unused stall holding an assortment of leather gear. There were no sidesaddles, but I had never cared for them when Lord Blacknall forced me to use them. My father had taught me to ride astride so I could cover ground more quickly when surveying our estates.

I found a couple of men's saddles in good repair and a number of bridles. I gave the horse a speculative look. He gazed back at me, unperturbed.

"No one will criticize me for riding astride if I only do it around Wishwood."

The horse nuzzled at the floor, finding leftover hay from Sebastian's horse.

I grimaced and hefted the saddle onto his back then tightened the cinches. The gelding made no complaint and took the bit without protest.

"Let's give this a try, boy, shall we?"

I put my foot in the stirrup and pulled myself up. The mammoth horse shifted but allowed me to guide him forward.

"You will need to have his feet attended to," said a heavily accented voice from behind me.

I twisted in the saddle to find Thomas's uncle Ignacio watching me. Up close, I saw the streaks of silver in his black hair and sharply pointed beard. He took a step closer, and I braced myself, my breath coming faster at the thought of being trapped in the stables with this lurking, scarred man. Could I convince the gelding to run? Or was I better off jumping down and fleeing on foot?

"I hope you will not scream at me again, *señora*." He smiled, which made his eyes twinkle with mischievous humor. I could see the resemblance to Thomas, though this uncle did not seem to carry the dark burden his nephew did.

"I..." I chuckled. "I will try not to if you try not to startle me."

Ignacio grinned. “I enjoy the outdoors and think of them as mine, but I do not intend to frighten ladies.” He paused and looked over horse and rider. “His hooves. You need to have them trimmed before you ride him.”

I exhaled slowly. “I was only seeing if he would carry me.”

“He will. My sister Castora brought him here.”

“From Spain.”

“The Spanish Netherlands.” He reached out, and the horse nuzzled his hand affectionately. Ignacio’s brow furrowed. “But this is strange. His hooves are very neat for how long he has been running free.”

“How long *has* he been running free?”

“Very long,” Ignacio said with a hint of sadness. He rubbed the horse’s forelock. “He is called Rocinante after the horse of my lord Alanso Quixano.”

“I don’t know your Alanso Quixano.”

He smiled. “You would not. He is from a book written in Spanish where he is called Don Quixote de La Mancha.”

“Oh. And the Don’s horse is a noble steed, I suppose.”

“A sad, broken nag until Don Quixote sees something different in him and gives him a noble name. What we are called matters, do you not think?”

I regarded him carefully. “I suppose it does. But I doubt I can say his name properly.”

“No, there is no music in the English tongue.” He shook his head. “I am sorry, but it is true. Do your best, and he will not mind. I will send for the village smith to check his feet.”

He turned away. It took a moment for me to follow the change in conversation.

“Thank you,” I called after him uncertainly, but he was already gone.

# Chapter Ten

That night, alone in my drafty room, I pulled a blanket around my shoulders and watched outside. Moonlight spilled over the pale gray ribs of the ruins, casting faint, arched shadows like grasping fingers across the gardens. I drew the blanket tighter around me.

A yellow glow, not from the moon, lit one side of the decaying church. It did not seem to come from the house. The faint light moved in the darkness, bobbing through the ruins. Goose pimples prickled over my skin. Another light followed close behind it. Then both blinked out.

I ducked away from the window in case whoever was out there could see me watching. Was this Thomas's ghost? But he insisted there was only one. A meeting of conspirators, then.

I was tempted to sneak downstairs and investigate, but I thought of twine tied across the stairs and falling stones and decided it would be wiser not to face an unknown number of faceless enemies alone. Instead, I huddled in my bed and pulled the curtains around me as if they could keep out more than the cold.

Faint creakings and whispers sighed through the black corridors of the house. Did the unknown visitors stay outside, or were they creeping through the corridors while the rest of the household slept? I sat up, alert for a cry of alarm or the smell of smoke, but only detected the faint scent of rosemary and an unnatural stillness. Intruders could be standing directly outside of my door and I would not know. Had I bolted it? If the nighttime visitors *were* ghostly, doors and bolts would not stop them.

I almost fled to Thomas's door to ask if he also saw the lights outside. If he heard strange noises in the house. But I would not give him the chance to mock me or turn me away. Instead, I opened the bed curtains just a crack and watched until my eyes grew too heavy.

The predawn chatter of birds roused me to the gray morning. The promise of a bright morning made my nighttime fears seem silly. I found my gown and slippers and made my way down the stairs—checking for twine—to the softly lit great hall. Faint clanking from the direction of the kitchen warned me that Hughes was already patrolling his domain. I tiptoed into the chapel.

Peaceful stillness settled over me as I sat in a well-polished pew and inhaled the faint perfume of rosemary and frankincense. The centuries-old sanctity of the chapel refused to be stirred by the troubles of the rest of the house, like a grand and elderly dame overlooking the silly squabbles and noise of a parcel of grandchildren. I studied the wood-paneled walls of the room and the silent pews and saw no sign that anyone else had used the room recently, though I knew there had been a secret meeting there several nights before.

Most of the chapel reflected a bare, Calvinist aesthetic, but one painted image hung on the wall: a bearded man wearing a bishop's miter. I looked more closely and saw a Latin name in the corner: Patricus. Patrick. St. Patrick again. The patron saint of Ireland?

Also painted on the wooden picture was an abbreviated prayer entitled "The Deer's Cry."

*I arise today*

*Through the power of Heaven,*

*The light of the sun,*

*The brilliance of the moon,*

*The splendor of fire,*

*The speed of lightning,*

*The swiftness of wind,*

*The depth of sea,*

*The firmness of earth.*

Lovely, but not entirely Christian, at least not to my ear. I puzzled over it for a moment, then stood.

The door leading out to the gardens was latched. If someone had been sneaking around in the house, they had an accomplice in Wishwood.

I stepped outside, searching the ground for signs of intruders. The hard-packed earth revealed nothing in the slow light of dawn, so I ventured farther, through the ruins and the gardens and into the woods.

In the distance, the sounds of Lord Blacknall's workers chopping trees broke the peace of the woods. I gave them a wide berth and came to a little meadow. Under the shade of a holly tree, I spotted my young friend Hal setting a snare. Beside him, an older boy stood offering Rocinante some grass—the same fair-haired lad who had thrown mud at my carriage and glared at me with such menace when I saw him spying on Lord Blacknall's workmen.

The horse perked up his ears and whickered at me. Both boys froze and turned in my direction.

I raised a hand in greeting. The older boy backed away, but Hal waved.

"Don't worry, Will," Hal said, "this is Lady Kate. She's the captive maiden I told you about. Lady Kate, this is my brother Will."

Will stared at me suspiciously. I bobbed a curtsey and smiled.

"We thought Hal was making up stories," Will said slowly. "You don't really live at Wishwood."

"I do. I think you would find it much different now than you've imagined it."

"But why would you be out in the woods?" Will asked. "I thought *gentle* folks had better things to do than scrounge out here."

"I'm hunting ghosts."

"In the daytime?" Hal wrinkled his nose.

"I thought I saw something outside last night." I studied both boys, with their tousled hair and clothes well-worn but in good repair. "You said everyone stays away from Wishwood, did you not?"

Hal nodded, his eyes wide, but Will frowned thoughtfully and said, "Everyone in the village does, but that's because there's rumors about odd things happening there. Witches and such." He gave me a challenging look. "Yet you claim to live there."

"I do. I'm no witch—"

"She's a proper noble lady!" Hal snapped at his brother.

I smiled gently. "My father was a baron. And I'm a good Christian woman, but I cannot say that nothing strange happens at Wishwood."

"Is it really haunted?" Hal asked.

"I don't know."

Hal pouted. "But it might be, then."

"As I said, 'tis a strange place. I was hoping you boys might know more about what happens in these woods."

Hal grinned. "I know the best places to catch rabbits, and I think I saw the highwayman once."

Will shot him an exasperated look.

Hal glared back at him and went on. "Our father might tell you more. He's lived here his whole life, and he's traveled around some, too. He knows everything," Hal added despairingly. A wise father must be a burden for an imaginative young lad.

"I would like to talk to him. Can you find out when I might meet him and leave a message for me at Wishwood?"

The boys exchanged looks.

"You want us to go to Wishwood?" Hal asked. "With the ghosts and wicked Lord Blacknall and all?"

"If you go in the daytime, you'll be safe." I thought of Hughes. "Though it might be best to come to the front door rather than the kitchen."

Will looked at me like I was mad, and Hal's eyes bugged.

"I know 'tis irregular, but so is everything else about Wishwood."

Hal nodded solemnly. "I'll do it."

"We'll see," Will added quickly. "We've learned not to trust those up at the house. We have to watch out for ourselves."

"Of course." I glanced down at the snares. Their father must have some idea of what they were doing out in the woods unless they cooked their hares spitted over a fire and never brought any home. But the elder Smithson might make a useful ally in the village.

Will noticed the direction of my gaze and jutted his chin out defiantly. "We do have to eat, after all. Hal said you did not mind us... being in the woods."

"I do not. In fact, I'm jealous that I don't know how to set a snare. Most days I only have porridge or eggs to eat."

"Really?" Hal glanced at his brother, who looked doubtful. "But that's what we eat too! I thought you'd eat roasted meat at every meal and great castles made of sugar and things."

I laughed. "If only that were true."

"I'll show you how to set a snare!" Hal offered.

Will shook his head, but I smiled at both of them. "That would be useful."

Will watched critically as Hal showed me how to lay a snare for a rabbit. At first, I was not sure I would actually do it, but as he guided me through the steps, I realized it would not be hard to add meat to our diet.

"We need to get home or Ma will miss us at breakfast," Will said.

Hal gave me a deep bow in farewell, and the two boys scurried off through the woods. Rocinante whickered and then trotted after them.

"Traitor," I said with a laugh. They must have spoiled him with treats from their garden.

I wandered back to the house, daydreaming about roast hare. Thomas would approve, or at least tolerate, my attempts to poach from Lord Blacknall. But what about Lord Blacknall's spy? I could use this as a chance to test the servants' loyalties. Lord Blacknall was as likely to be amused as angry if I were caught poaching a single rabbit from him, so it was not much of a risk.

I gathered some roses from the garden and braved the kitchen entrance. Mistress Hughes did not even look up from her pot. I fed my yeast starter fresh flour and water and spotted a glazed white vase decorated with blue vines and fruit. Perfect for the roses. I took it with me, hoping Thomas had not already lost himself in his study.

I bumped into Hughes in the doorway. He glared, his faded eyes bulging.

"And what are you interfering with now?" he snapped.

I held up the flowers and vase. "Breakfast, I suppose. What else have I interfered with?"

"You and your kind are always meddling."

He shuffled past me before I could ask what "my kind" were. Did he mean women? Perhaps Castora Westwood had not been as passive as I imagined. At any rate, Mistress Hughes was lucky to be deaf if her husband spoke like that to her.

I ventured into the corridor and stopped short. Thomas was waiting at the table in front of his study. He glanced up at me.

"You are late."

"You... you waited for me."

"We had an arrangement."

His gaze fell on the vase and he frowned.

"I thought our meal needed some cheer," I said, setting the vase in the center of the table between our two bowls of oat gruel.

"That's a majolica vase from Barcelona. 'Tis quite old."

"Oh," I said stupidly. I moved to take the flowers out of it, but Thomas waved my hand away.

"Never mind. No point in trying to make it last forever." He took a bite of the gruel and swallowed it with some effort. "How is that fresh bread of yours coming along?"

I grinned. "I'll be able to bake some soon."

"That's good news. And how is Sara working out as your maid?"

"She doesn't spend the night in the house."

"I made different arrangements for her. Is that a problem?"

"'Tis only strange." And lonely, but I could not tell him that. "But she's cheerful and hard-working."

"I'm glad to hear it." He glanced again at the vase. "I did not know we had roses this time of year."

"It looks like they have been blooming for some weeks."

"My mother was fond of the gardens, but I never pay much attention to them, I'm afraid."

I frowned at that. Had Margaret not said that her master liked her to tend the gardens? "What do you pay attention to? What are you working on in your study?"

He did not answer for a moment, then shrugged one shoulder. "I am translating the texts in the library. Making an English copy of each one."

I stared at him in surprise. "How many languages do you know?"

"Four. Or five. My German is not very good."

I knew my husband was no fool, but I did not guess he was such a scholar. It made me feel a bit shy and anxious to impress him. "My father taught me French. We used to practice as we rode the grounds at Aubrey Hall." I paused at the stab in my chest and pushed away my memories of home. "How did you learn?"

"Tío Ignacio taught me."

"How did *he* learn so many?"

Thomas's eyes brightened in amusement. "He started with Spanish."

I smiled and shook my head. "That's impressive. You're translating all of those books? Why?"

"Is it not a worthy pursuit?"

"Aye, but, of all things..."

"Oh. I started just reading them. Looking for answers. But then I decided if I had to translate them anyway, in my head, I should write them out. Leave a... a legacy of sorts."

"That's commendable. And impressive." I ran my thumb over the smooth pewter of the spoon. "Do you... do you think your time is very short?"

Thomas's arm jerked, and he grimaced. I looked up in alarm. "My lord?"

"I'm fine. But, were you really out so early just to gather flowers for our table?"

"I was also exploring a little." I paused and met his curious gaze. "Do you ever see strange things outside at night?"

"I sleep heavily." He tilted his head. "What kind of strange things?"

"Lights in the darkness."

His lips quirked. "The ghost?"

"Only if there are more than one and they come into the house."

His brow furrowed, and he looked down. "Hmm."

"I wonder if we are all in danger. If there are bandits sneaking into the house at night."

"I don't think whatever spirits you may be seeing mean us any harm."

He knew something. "I thought you said there was only one ghost."

He lashed his arm out, smacking the vase. The vase rocked, but I caught it before it crashed onto the stone floor. Thomas clutched his arm to his chest.

"Are you injured, my lord?" I asked.

"It is nothing," he said stiffly. "This meal is at an end."

He pushed back his chair and stormed into his study, slamming the door. I rose and set the vase back in its place, my hands chilled, though I did not understand why.

# Chapter Eleven

Thomas made no mention of the vase or ghosts at breakfast the next day, or for the rest of the week. Indeed, he barely spoke to me at all, even when I finally served him warm bread made from my starter.

And why should that sting me? Let him keep his secrets. I would find out on my own who else at Wishwood had something to hide: secret meetings in the night and a reason to harm Thomas or me. I checked the latches before I retired to bed and kept my door bolted, but I still itched with the sensation that someone unseen was watching me.

I tried to spy on Sebastian, but my husband's cousin remained as slippery as a greased weasel. One early morning, when I stepped out to check if any of my snares had caught some meat for the table, I spotted him in the stable, pulling the saddle from his horse. At his belt hung a heavy bag of coins. I raised my eyebrows and crept back out of sight.

It was not an idle boast, perhaps, when he said he could help me sue out my livery. But where did the money come from? There was no honest employment for a gentleman in this neighborhood, but the villagers told stories of a highwayman.

And Sebastian and Thomas were not the only ones with secrets.

Several days later, as Sara dreamily scooped the ashes from the fireplace in the great hall, Margaret came up behind her and poked her with the broom bristles. "What's taking you so long? Are you drawing in the ashes to see who you'll marry?"

"Ha! *You* might need devil's tricks like that, but not *me*."

Margaret's eyes narrowed. "Foolish child."

Sara straightened and clenched her fists. "I am not!"

"Girls!" I stepped in. "What's this about?"

They shared a nasty look and then studied the floor, refusing to meet my eyes.

"Very well," I said. "Back to work, both of you."

"Sorry, m'lady," Margaret mumbled.

Sara kept her eyes down, her lashes low as though she was holding back tears. Certainly not because of my scolding. Margaret's insult must have hit a nerve.

I watched Margaret out of the corner of my eye as I secured an oiled cloth over a broken window pane. As soon as she thought I was distracted, she snuck off through the chapel. The woman reminded me of a cat, always prowling about the garden. Everything about it made me suspect she had a man on the side. Who would that be? One of the discontented villagers? Or was she Lord Blacknall's spy?

I was studying my opponent's move on the chessboard when Sara ran up to the gallery, her cheeks bright red.

"What is it, Sara?"

"There's a... young man here to see you, mistress."

"To see me?"

She nodded. I rushed down the stairs behind her.

Hal stood in the great hall, gawking at the mostly empty room and shifting from foot to foot.

"My lady," he said, bowing deeply. "You need to come."

"What's the matter?"

"There's a disturbance in the village. An argument between the workers and the villagers, and no one to stop it. Pa says it will turn into a riot."

I placed a hand on his trembling shoulder. "You did right to come here. Tell your father someone from the manor will be there to quell the fighting."

I rushed to pound on the door of Thomas's study.

"Go away!" he called through the door.

"You are needed!"

He swung the door open. "What is going on?"

"There's a riot in the village. You need to stop it."

"Me?" He looked both annoyed and amused by the suggestion. "Blacknall has taken that power from my hands. Let him deal with it."

I grabbed the door before he could shut it. "You cannot stop Lord Blacknall from enclosing the woods, but you can help the villagers settle their disputes. God has placed you in a position to oversee them."

"God has placed me in a position to be useless to them. Let the villagers drive out Blacknall's men. They have my full approval."

"Lord Blacknall's men are better armed. The villagers will suffer."

Thomas's brow furrowed, and he looked away. "Why don't you settle it, then?"

"The landowner's wife is not the proper person to do so. But I would accompany you and offer my advice if you wanted it."

He studied me. "What a fitting helpmeet you would be."

I nodded and held out a hand for him. He reached toward me, then curled his fingers into a fist and shook his head.

"'Tis a shame it is wasted on me," he said quietly.

"It does not have to be." I did my best to keep my voice level, trying not to shout at him for his stubbornness. For the way his rejection cut like a rapier to my chest. "I am your wife."

"And I give you permission to do as you think best."

I released the door, tempted to slam it in his face. Impossible man! He left me no choice. I would quell the riot myself. I dashed outside and found Rocinante, luring him to the stable so I could saddle him. I would have to ride astride, like a man, but in this situation, it might give me more authority.

As I cantered down the lane, Sebastian rode up beside me.

"Where are you going?" he asked.

"To stop a riot," I snapped over my shoulder.

"Excellent idea."

He brought his steed into pace with mine. I wanted to shoo him away, but he might be helpful this time. We reined in at the end of the lane where a group of villagers and workers had fallen to blows.

Sebastian drew a pistol and fired it off.

The fighting immediately came to a standstill, and the groups drew apart, giving us wary looks.

"You handle the villagers, and I'll calm the workers," Sebastian said.

I did not like taking orders from him, but his idea was sound.

I trotted Rocinante over to the villagers, who stared up at me in something akin to awe.

"Who are you, then?" one of them called.

"I am Lady Katherine Westwood. I am here representing my husband, Thomas Westwood."

There was a good deal of mumbling. I caught, "Witch's boy."

"The lunatic?" one man asked.

"He is not. His health is poor, which prevents him from coming himself, but his mind is sound."

One of the men nodded and gestured at me. "My boy Hal's been telling stories about a golden-haired lady held captive at the old priory." He met my eyes. "It sounds like she's been a friend to Hal."

So, this was Master Smithson, who might be my best connection to the village. Will was there beside him, and he glared at me with undisguised mistrust.

I met Smithson's eyes. "I would be a friend to all of you. Lord Blacknall is my guardian, but I am no ally of his. I want to see order restored here."

A few of the men nodded with a range of wariness and hope. Several eyed me while whispering to each other, Will among them.

"But we cannot have order if you fight with Lord Blacknall's men," I said. "For the moment, they have the right to be here. I know Lord Blacknall has trampled your traditional rights, and my husband and I are doing everything in our power to regain control of these lands from Lord Blacknall. When we do, we will restore your rights to use the woods."

More wariness. More hope. It hurt me to see it. I had to find a way to keep my promise.

The men slowly dispersed, and I turned Rocinante back. The workers had retreated into the woods. Sebastian was waiting for me, a smirk curling his lips.

"Not bad, for a female."

"And I managed it without a pistol," I shot back.

He laughed. "Yes, with false promises. Even more deadly. But don't worry, when Wishwood is mine, I'll treat the tenants better than Lord Blacknall does. 'Tis in my interest, after all. His lordship only sees the immediate value of the wood and forgets about the long-term value of the people and their lands."

"What a benevolent tyrant you would be. Too bad you will never have the opportunity." I wanted to be sure of that, both to spite him and for the sake of the villagers.

"Don't fear, my lady. I make opportunities."

With that, he galloped away. I glared after him, willing his horse to stumble and throw him. But he was a skilled rider. A highwayman would have to be. And the pistol would help too. When I looked over my shoulder, I saw many of the village men watching Sebastian's back, their eyes full of hate.

I looked back to where Sebastian had disappeared. Was it possible I was looking at this wrong, and someone wanted Sebastian out of the way? A man like him must have enemies. If someone made it look like Sebastian had killed his cousin, Sebastian would hang. There might be someone who would benefit from having both Thomas and Sebastian gone, or Thomas could be expendable in getting to Sebastian. As I rode back to Wishwood, I wondered if the threat was waiting for me at the house, or if I was leaving the real danger behind me.

# Chapter Twelve

As I brushed Rocinante, the desperate hope on the villagers' faces haunted me. Without leadership, they would band together to protect themselves from whatever they saw as a threat, whether that was Lord Blacknall or Wishwood.

I groaned and leaned against Rocinante's warmth. He flicked me with his tail.

"Oh, go on then." I gave him a gentle slap, and he trotted toward the woods.

I climbed up the stairs above the stables to the walkway and found the spot where the stone had nearly fallen on Thomas and me. I rested my hand on a worn arch. The stones did not shift, even when I gave a half-hearted shove. I peered down at the ground below. Someone had been angry to have the strength to push that stone over. And someone had been lurking about to have the opportunity.

The door to the gallery opened, and I jumped. Thomas stepped onto the walkway, watching me curiously. I gave him a shallow curtsey.

"I take it you succeeded in calming the villagers," he said.

"You could have done the same."

"But I could not have." He leaned against one of the arches and studied the stones, his eyes troubled. "What did the villagers say?"

"They're angry about Lord Blacknall's men. And I had to assure them you're not a lunatic."

He smiled thinly. "A waste of breath. They have already decided."

"Because you have nothing to do with them."

"That was not my choice. What have you heard about my mother?"

"Pardon?" I asked cautiously.

He met my eyes, demanding the truth. "What have you heard?"

"There seem to be some rumors that she... she was a witch. I do not believe them. Sara speaks well of her, and in her picture, she looks kind."

Of course, there was no grave marker for her next to his father.

"I lost my mother when I was young, too," I added. "I barely remember her, but I would hate to hear such things about her."

"Aye." Thomas was quiet for a moment, and his expression softened. He strode down the walkway and turned back to me. "This is where they say it happened."

"What?"

"My mother," he whispered and looked over the edge.

I walked down to stand next to him and peer over the low stone railing at the garden below. "Do you mean she fell?"

"I was not there, but that's not the story I've been told. They say she was fleeing from some unseen terror. She screamed and fell over the edge."

"I'm so sorry." What a terrible way to lose a mother. What a terrible way to die.

Thomas smiled sadly. "Ah, but that's not the end of the tale. As she fell, she cried out a prayer, and her body transformed into a white bird..."

A shiver prickled down my back. "The owl."

He met my eyes. "Aye, the owl. Proof that she was in league with the devil."

"Or with God."

Thomas shrugged.

"And who witnessed this transformation?"

"Supposedly my father, though he would not speak of what he saw. And one or two servants who are no longer living. In fact, everyone who might have told me what truly happened that night is dead. I have no idea if the story is true or the product of minds deranged by grief. But word spread quickly. She was foreign. She had cried out strange words before her fall. She was a witch."

Witches were not buried on holy ground.

Neither were suicides.

Thomas went on. "All she left behind was a grieving husband who did not live much longer and a sickly boy whom the villagers condemned as a lunatic and left to the not-so-tender mercies of his lordship. You see, the villagers have no interest in listening to me, and I have no interest in forcing them to after the things they've said about my mother. Let Blacknall strip the place clean. The villagers can move to the city, this place can rot to the ground, and perhaps its sad history can be forgotten."

I stepped closer and put a hand on his arm. He straightened, reminding me how tall he was. How intimidating, when he stared down at me with those almost-black eyes. That was the only reason my heart was beating so quickly and my throat had gone dry.

"You should leave me in peace," Thomas said, but he did not move away from me.

I stared into his dark eyes. "That does not please me."

He whisked a stray lock off my shoulder. I shivered pleasantly where his fingers brushed warm and light over my skin.

"And what does please you?" he asked, his voice low.

"Your... your hair."

"My hair?" Amusement sparkling in his eyes.

"The way you have styled it. 'Tis fetching."

I touched a strand of his black locks, then stroked my finger down it. His gaze traveled along the edge of my face, down to my throat, where my pulse quickened, and finally back to my lips. I leaned in, and Thomas placed a hand cautiously on my waist, pulling me closer. Perhaps he had not forgotten our kiss after all. He brought his face so close to mine that his warm breath brushed my cheek.

He paused and slowly pushed away, shaking his head.

I had trouble finding my breath. "My lord?"

"This is not right." He turned his gaze down to me, his dark eyes wary. "This is not what you wanted. Unless... you want to make sure the marriage is legal and you get an heir. Save your precious Aubrey Hall."

"This"—I gestured between us—"is not about that! Is it too much to believe I want us to be happy together?"

"There is no happiness here. Wishwood is cursed. If you got your heir, the child would be cursed too."

A sob caught in my throat, but I forced it down. "It does not have to be so."

Thomas shook his head and turned his back on me. "Curses do not care what we want. Take heart, though. You will have Blacknall's backing when I'm gone."

"And why is that?" I snapped.

"If Sebastian inherits, Blacknall loses control of the lands."

"I might wrest control of Wishwood from Lord Blacknall as a widow."

"Only if you can sue out your livery."

I frowned. "Certainly, you have some say in what would happen. A will?"

He laughed mirthlessly. "Drawn up by Blacknall's lawyers."

"And your father's will? The deeds to the land?"

"Conveniently missing."

I narrowed my eyes. "For how long?"

"Since my father's death, to the best of my knowledge."

Convenient indeed.

Thomas looked out through the archway to the overgrown cloister gardens below. "Once I'm gone, Blacknall will arrange to give you back your father's lands, and in return, you'll allow him to strip Wishwood to the bone."

"Never!"

"Would you not?"

"I have seen the suffering he causes."

"And he will threaten your lands with the same. Will you allow him to do it?"

I opened my mouth to deny it, but the words would not come. Becca and everyone at Aubrey Hall depended on me. But

I had just made a promise to the people in the village, too. My father's recklessness had left Aubrey Hall in my hands, Thomas's caution would do the same with Wishwood, and I was just one person. Was there any way to save all of them? Not alone.

"Help me defy him!"

"Don't you see?" Thomas took a step back from me. "It is all out of our hands. Find something that gives you a sense of purpose—something that you *can* control—and forget about the rest of it or you will make yourself mad."

He left me to think over his words. Something I *could* control? Why could I not make him see past his fear of curses and predestination? I thumped my fists against a stone arch and then stared at my hands, rough and red from scrubbing and mending. My eyes stung, but I squeezed them shut and pinched the bridge of my nose. I could not afford to break down. Not when I was all alone. When everything rested on me.

I trudged back inside and sat heavily by the chessboard. My opponent had moved his knight forward. It was not threatening any of my pieces yet, but knights were tricky, able to move suddenly and threaten unexpected attacks. If I took his knight, it would leave my bishop exposed to his queen. Would he risk his queen for the sake of a bishop?

As I sat contemplating my next move, Sara walked by with an armful of clean linens. She paused to curtsey, looking at the chessboard with vague interest.

"I'm glad everything is calm again, my lady," she said.

"As am I. Have you ever had any trouble with the villagers?"

Her smile faded. "I did back when... well, but not anymore. They just leave me alone now."

"What changed?"

Sara looked uncomfortable and shrugged. "Just being at Wishwood. We're safe here."

I was skeptical of that. Villagers elsewhere had rioted when their lands were enclosed, and Thomas had no friendly relations with his neighbors. In fact, Wishwood was beginning to seem an especially dangerous place to be.

Sara hurried off to finish her work. The damaged picture of Castora Westwood watched me from the wall. She could not be a witch. Had she gone mad and thrown herself off the walkway?

I left the chessboard as it was for the time being and returned to my room to study the torn painting of Thomas. Perhaps it was unfinished because his mother had died during its creation. That would mean he had been about the same age I was when I lost my mother. I tried to smooth the ragged edges of the canvas together, but if I glued them that way, there would be a nasty gash across his face. I did not want that.

A bang echoed from Thomas's room.

"My lord?" I called.

No answer.

I tapped lightly on his door and swung it open. The room was empty, but the bed curtains swayed as though someone had stood by them just a moment before.

"Thomas?" I asked.

Nothing.

But someone had just been in the room, I was sure. There were two doors on the opposite side of his room. Thomas would not hide from me, would he? I doubted it. I opened the first door. A closet full of linens and moth-eaten blankets, tossed aside haphazardly as though someone had dug through them.

I left everything as I found it and moved to the next closet. I opened the door, and a dark shadow moved toward me.

I tried to scream as a hand wrapped around my throat. A masked man loomed over me. I reached up under his hood and grabbed a handful of hair, yanking hard. The masked man gave a muffled shout and released my throat. I screamed shrilly, still holding tight to the man's hair. I brought my foot down hard on his, and he jerked back, tearing his hair loose from my hand.

The figure disappeared in the dark shadows of the rear of the closet. This was no ghost, though. I still held his hair in my hand. I stumbled forward, feeling my way. Cold air whisked past me, and the back of the closet never appeared. I fumbled into open air until my foot came down hard on a stair. I caught myself against a stone wall. Secret stairs in the back of the closet? I felt my way down, trying to stay quiet while I clung to the wall.

I reached the bottom, and light spilled in to brighten my last few steps. I'd come out through a doorway concealed in the wood-paneled wall of the chapel.

Ignacio stood in the door leading to the great hall, staring at me.

"You!" I said.

He looked confused. "Me?"

"'Twas you just now. You are the intruder!"

"Have you been having a nightmare, *doña*?"

I uncurled my fist. The hairs in my hand glittered golden under the rushlights. Not Ignacio. Not even Sebastian.

Ignacio came to examine what I was looking at. "Something has pulled out your hair?"

The blond strands *were* close to my own color. "Nay, someone attacked me, and I pulled out his hair. He fled through here."

"I heard a commotion," Ignacio said, "but there was no one here when I arrived."

I glanced around the dim chapel. The door leading to the gardens stood open.

Ignacio ran through and glanced out, but he shook his head. "He is gone." He bolted the door and came back to me.

"You say this man attacked you? Here in the house?"

"He was in Thomas's chamber. I do not know if he was trying to rob him. He seemed to be lying in wait."

"To rob him?" Ignacio's eyes narrowed. "Or to harm him?"

I nodded numbly. Someone was trying to kill my husband, and it was not his uncle or his cousin. Unless they had hired someone else to do it. The local highwayman, assuming it was not Sebastian after all? In fact, the townspeople hated Thomas too. Almost anyone could be trying to kill him.

# Chapter Thirteen

I studied the blond hairs in my hand. Will Smithson had fair hair. I could not remember if he was taller than me, but his father was the local blacksmith, and if he was following his father's trade, he would be strong.

"Thomas needs to know," I said.

Ignacio nodded. "We will tell him."

We walked to the study, and Ignacio tapped on the door.

"What is it?" Thomas's annoyance was clear through the door.

"We need to speak to you, *mi sobrino*," Ignacio called

Thomas opened the door and glared at us with mistrust. Ignacio glanced at me, and I straightened.

"Someone tried to attack you," I said.

"You found another trap?" Thomas looked faintly amused.

"Nay. They attacked me. In your room. I pulled out their hair." I showed him the golden locks. He glanced at my hair and then at his uncle.

"I heard the struggle but saw no one," Ignacio said.

"They were robbing you. Or lying in wait for you."

Thomas frowned. "I will consider this."

He shut the door on us.

I wanted to scream at him, but instead, I stormed up to the gallery. On my way, I passed Margaret, who clutched a bundle of carrots from the garden. She watched me with wide eyes. Well, the servants were bound to know eventually, and perhaps they should be aware of the danger lurking in Wishwood.

Ignacio found me upstairs a few minutes later, staring at the chessboard.

"The bishop is a powerful piece," Ignacio said.

"Aye, but the knight can take you unawares."

He sat across from me. "There was a disturbance in the village?"

"A fight between the villagers and Lord Blacknall's workmen. Sebastian and I broke it up. I wish I could convince Thomas to get involved, but he does not seem to care." About the village, about his safety, about me.

"I want to take him away from here," Ignacio said, his dark eyes angry. "Yet I have nowhere to go. I do not understand why this Lord Blacknall is his guardian, who does not care for him. I suppose it is because I am Spanish."

"You truly don't understand?" I looked at him with sympathy. "It is because his ancestor who bought this land bought it from the king. Sometimes people were able to get the land more freely, but often it came with a promise of knight-service."

"Thomas is not a knight, nor was his father."

"He's not. It is a... a trick the king used to make his landowners dependent on him—to get money."

"The root of all evil!"

"It does seem that way. But it means that the king has an interest—part ownership if you will—in Thomas and his lands."

"Is this why strangers come and steal our timber?"

"It is. The king has given the care of Thomas and his lands over to Lord Blacknall. He did the same with mine."

"This is not right."

"It is not. Some people find a way to protect their children..." I stopped as an old ache twinged in my chest. My father had not even tried to make some provision to hide me from the king's searchers. If he was going to be rash with his own life, he at least could have been thoughtful of mine.

Ignacio frowned. "Peter, my sister's husband, he was a good man. A good father. I do not understand why he would leave Thomas in this situation. I know he wanted me to care for my nephew."

"Perhaps he did not know about the conditions of his landholding. Or maybe he thought Wishwood would be overlooked." Could he have hidden the missing deed, trying to protect his son?

"He was always cautious. Like Thomas. Marrying Castora was perhaps the only adventurous thing he ever did." Ignacio smiled sadly, then clenched his fist. "I must protect my nephew. He is all the family I have left."

"We will find out who is trying to harm Thomas," I said.

Ignacio gave me a long look. "I am glad you came here. You care about Thomas."

"I suppose I do," I said softly. "I'm afraid he does not care much for me, though."

"Perhaps his heart is afraid," Ignacio said. "Someday you may coax it out."

I nodded, but I was not convinced. Ignacio left me to my game. I moved my knight to threaten my opponent's queen, leaving his knight on the board and keeping my bishop safe.

That evening, as Sara brushed out my hair before bed, I watched our reflections in the window. She wore her usually dreamy expression, but when the owl hooted outside, her smile froze, and her hands paused.

"Sara?" I asked.

She forced a smile. "Sorry, my lady. 'Tis just the owl... sometimes it..." She met my eyes in our reflection, then looked away. "It sounds silly."

"You can tell me." Had she heard the story of Thomas's mother?

"It sounds so lonely. Sometimes I think it is trying to warn me about something. Shakes me to the core, it does." She stared past our reflections to the darkness gathering outside.

"Do you think you are in danger, walking home in the dark? The villagers—"

"Oh, nay! 'Tis not that! Only, sometimes it gives me a deep chill. All that loneliness in the dark. Like that's all that's waiting for us out there." Sara shook herself. "But then I remember that I just have to let go. To trust. Everything will be taken care of. 'Twill turn out right."

She smiled beatifically and resumed her brushing.

After she bid me goodnight and left me alone, I still stared out the window. The owl called again. I blew out my candle, and as my eyes adjusted to the darkness, I caught a light moving out in the ruins. Ghost or not, it did not seem to bother Sara. I would not let it bother me any longer.

I slipped on my robe and boots and snuck out after Sara. I took the kitchen door, not wanting a direct confrontation with someone coming in through the chapel. Nothing moved in the dusky gloom except for Sara's slender form, so I followed her. She walked into the gathering twilight, humming her way through the mists curling up around the ruins.

The stars above reminded me of my childhood. Strange how they stayed the same while all else changed. My father had taught me their names and how some people believed they controlled our destinies. We had scoffed together at such an idea, but now I looked up at the pinpricks of light and wished there was someone to share this burden with me. That I did not feel constantly crushed by the needs of everyone else, with no one to offer a word of comfort for me. To feel my father's reassuring embrace.

Or my husband's.

I shook my head. I was alone.

On the far side of the ruins, I noticed an old caretaker's cottage with a warm glow coming from its windows—Sara's destination. She opened the door to go inside, admitting a quick flash of light to the nighttime. I crept up to peer in the window. Fitting with what I had predicted for the girl, Sara kissed an old woman on her wrinkled cheek and sat to gaze fondly at her and chatter about her day.

A small boy with raven-black curls threw himself onto Sara, disrupting the scene that fit so well with what I had first imagined. She embraced and kissed him and held him on her lap, stroking his head as she babbled on to the nodding woman.

The older woman was far beyond child-bearing years. This child was Sara's. And she was young herself and gave no sign that she had ever been married. If she were, she likely would not be working all day as a maid while her mother or grandmother watched her child.

I took one last long look at the dark-haired boy. Thomas knew about this arrangement—he said he had come up with it. He took little interest in the dealings of his household, but Sara was unusually loyal to such a distant master.

Unless he was not as distant as I had thought.

I scurried back through the ruins, my stomach as heavy as an iron pot. Was Thomas uninterested in me because he had fallen in love with one of his servants? I should not let it affect me. Many of our station married for convenience and found love elsewhere. It was rational, I supposed, yet the thought revolted me.

I paused, finding myself in the old priory cemetery. I stepped carefully past a couple of decaying wooden markers. They belonged to the past and had no bearing on my problems now. But as I made my way through the ruins, I glanced up to find the barn owl watching me, and I felt, like Sara, that it was trying to warn me of secrets I could not see.

Something else moved in the shadows, coming toward me. Two figures. I hid behind a crumbling archway and watched them pass. The first was clearly Ignacio creeping away from Wishwood in the middle of the night. I did not recognize the second figure. Maybe someone from the village?

I sank down into the damp grass clinging around the stones. Ignacio seemed sincerely interested in protecting his nephew, but what if I was wrong? Margaret and Sara both had young men on the side, it appeared, though such behavior was not usually tolerated among servants. Old Hughes was oddly protective of his wife and her domain in the kitchen. Sebastian had villainy written on his features. And the villagers were angry with Lord Blacknall and with Wishwood—including blond-haired Will.

Why was I troubling myself over Wishwood's problems? Thomas did not want my help. He did not want me. But I had made a promise. I pushed myself up from the cold ground and picked my way back to the house. While passing through the kitchen, I heard scuffling footsteps in the corridor.

I peeked out to see Margaret entering her chamber in the servants' area. She once again clutched her lace handkerchief, but this time, instead of looking sad, her face was set in anger or frustration. I pulled back until her door slammed.

As I tiptoed past, the sounds of muffled sobs made me pause. She would not welcome my intrusion, but I ached to hear anyone so upset. Had she had a falling out with a male friend? Or, was she forced to do something she did not want to, maybe by Lord Blacknall? Careful not to disturb her grief, I hurried back to my room.

# Chapter Fourteen

The next morning, I found a folded paper slipped under my door.

> *Naughty Katherine,*
>
> *My agent tells me you are not minding your needlework like a good girl, but instead snooping in Wishwood's past. If you must do so, spend your time finding the missing deed. With that, we might work out an arrangement that would benefit you. Your dear Becca sends her greetings.*
>
> *Blacknall*

Lord Blacknall and his spy! I had only spoken to Thomas about the deed, but someone had been listening. And Lord Blacknall wanted the deed enough to both bargain with me and threaten Becca over it. Would it hurt Wishwood for him to have the deed? That all depending on what was in it. Thomas questioned what I would do if I had to choose between Aubrey Hall and Wishwood. Lord Blacknall offered me the chance to find out.

I wadded the paper to toss in the fireplace, then I pictured Becca thrown out onto the streets alone, my mother's rooms leased to some stranger, our tenants starving because Lord Blacknall enclosed their woods and fields. I smoothed the letter out and tucked it behind the tapestry before descending to the great hall for breakfast.

Thomas arrived a few minutes later, his eyes underlined by dark circles.

He looked at the table and shook his head. "I passed the night poorly. I will not be eating this morning."

I decided not to argue, but stood and moved the table away. Thomas looked a little surprised that I relented so easily, but I could not force him to befriend me. And if his heart was set elsewhere... well, it made no difference if I ate with him or not.

He unlocked his study and walked in. I turned away. I would eat alone in the gallery. A moment later, Thomas jogged back out. My heart lifted a little. Had he changed his mind?

But he ran past me and grabbed a rapier from the display on the wall. I sucked in a deep breath and looked around for the attacker to show himself. Thomas rushed back to his study. I tried to peek in after him, but he shooed me away.

"Stand back!"

I pressed against the wall. He strode out with the sword held straight out in front of him, a long snake dangling from the end. Its head was marked by a "V."

"Door," he called to me.

I ran ahead of him to open the door, and he tossed the snake free.

I shut the door and turned to him. "What—"

"An adder. It would have been unfortunate for me if I had not spotted it before I put my hand down."

"How did it get in your study?"

"Excellent question. They usually stay in the woods or garden."

"It could have been forced under the door."

"Possibly."

I huffed. "I suppose you think it slithered in there because you're cursed."

"It does seem that God is trying to put a period to my existence."

"God! He could do it more effectively. This is the work of man."

Thomas returned the sword to its place. "Perhaps."

"You are ready to accept that someone is trying to hurt you?"

Thomas lapsed into a vacant stare, his mouth moving silently, then he blinked and looked back at me. "I don't know. 'Tis hard for me to see the motivation for all this effort."

"Sebastian has one."

He sighed. "Sebastian has the devil's own patience. And I have work to do." He walked back into his study and shut the door.

I growled under my breath and stormed upstairs to the gallery, where I found Sebastian picking at his bread and butter.

"Why are you doing this?" I asked.

He raised an eyebrow. "Silly goose, to wonder why I enjoy her excellent household management. The food has improved since my cousin married. I'll have to spend even more time here." He grinned.

"And that's why you're trying to kill Thomas?"

"Kill him? Not at all. I'm willing to wait."

"Someone put an adder in his study."

"An adder?" Sebastian stood and paced to the wall to look at the pictures. "How oddly ineffective for an assassin."

"Ineffective?"

"Adders are toxic, but not always deadly. If my cousin was bitten by one, though, a physician would be needed."

"Of course. It would be expensive, but I'm sure Lord Blacknall would pay. He would have to."

Sebastian raised an eyebrow and smirked. "How little you know. I appreciate your mercenary outlook, but not everything is about money."

"Then what?"

"Ask your husband. But I am concerned that someone outside our little family is taking such an interest in our affairs."

He bowed and exited across the walkway. Was Sebastian truly concerned? Maybe, if it interfered with whatever he was scheming.

I sat at the chessboard and studied the pieces, but my mind was not on the game. I twirled the queen in her place. Lord Blacknall did not want me to snoop into the past, so that was what I had to do.

I trotted downstairs and tapped on the study door. "My lord?"

No answer.

"Thomas?" I called.

"Leave me!" came the muffled voice from behind the door.

"I will not," I said. "I have something to discuss with you."

Thomas flung the door open. "What is it?"

"A delicate matter."

He rolled his eyes and gestured me into his study, shutting the door on any eavesdroppers. "Now, what is too delicate to discuss in front of a few nearly-deaf old servants?"

"I need the truth."

"The truth?" Thomas glanced at his books. "Don't we all?"

"I mean about Wishwood. I am tired of secrets."

"Then I wish Blacknall had sent you elsewhere."

I flinched from his words but rallied myself. "Perhaps it would help if I understood where I stand at Wishwood."

"Where you stand?" His expression grew more guarded. "I thought it was obvious. You're free to do whatever you like."

"As are you?"

He laughed drily. "Apparently not, since all I wish to do is work in peace."

"And yet, if you have a mistress, it would be better for it to be acknowledged between us. Less awkward."

Thomas looked startled for a moment, and then he broke into sincere laughter. "A mistress? And I'm keeping her here at Wishwood, I suppose?"

"I know that Sara has a child, and she is very loyal to you."

He sobered quickly. "Ah, that. You've been prying. And you assume the child is mine, and that I'm so shabby that I would make this infamous offspring of mine live in a run-down cottage, and my beloved mistress sleep under a different roof?"

I flushed. "I would assume you had a reason—"

"Stop assuming so much."

"You tell me nothing."

"True enough." He turned his chair to face me and sat. "I was aware that Sara has a child. The creature is not mine, and I would never intrude on Sara's innocence."

"Innocence? But—"

"Oh, she has a child, so there's a certain level of innocence lost, to be sure. But you would have to be an idiot not to see what a naive little waif Sara is." He leaned forward. "You will not intrude on it either."

I stepped back from his challenging gaze. "I am only trying to look out for myself, and for you."

"I keep telling you not to."

"I am your wife. Perhaps it is not what either of us planned or wished, but I made a vow, and—"

"Hang your vows," he growled.

"I will do no such thing. You may believe all the Calvinist drivel you like, but God holds us accountable—"

Thomas stood. "No one should be held accountable for a vow they were forced to take."

"I was not forced. I was pressed, I admit, but it was my choice."

"You did not fully understand." He turned away, flipping through the pages of one of his books. "You were deceived."

"Deceived? How?"

"You were tricked into a marriage with someone who never should have been allowed to marry at all."

My forehead wrinkled. "How so?" A horrifying thought made me blush. "You are already married!"

"Nothing of the sort." He snapped the book shut. Then his eyes went vague again, and he moved his mouth as though trying to speak but unable.

I rubbed my arms and backed against the wall. His eyes focused on me again.

"I'm not going to hurt you," Thomas said softly. "At least not on purpose. I told you I was cursed."

"Superstition," I mumbled.

"Whatever you might think of Wishwood's witches and ghosts, there is one truth you cannot avoid: I am an epileptic."

"Epileptic?"

"I have the falling evil," Thomas said, not meeting my eyes. "I ought to be locked in a hospital. If Blacknall had not covered it up to use me for his schemes, I would be. I certainly would not be allowed to marry." He met my gaze, his dark eyes unreadable. "So, you see, you were deceived. I would never hold you to your vows. If I were able, I would sue out your livery and let you go live in freedom on your estate."

I stared at him, absorbing what he was telling me. "Your mind is sound."

"Sound enough, I suppose. But I'm afflicted by some evil, so I am sometimes not in control of myself."

I took a step back.

Thomas shook his head. "I don't mean that I do anything violent. But my own limbs act against my will, as you have seen at breakfast. And sometimes my mind goes... I know not where." His voice caught. "Certainly, if there were some sign of God's displeasure, this would be it. I am the child of a witch, from a cursed family, and I will never be a fit husband. I am not even fit to rule my own household."

I pursed my lips. "Only for lack of effort. Is there not a tale in the Bible, where the men say the man born blind must have sinned, and Jesus said it was not because of sin but to show forth God's power?"

Thomas shook his head. "This is no Bible story. This is my life and yours. My body and mind don't belong entirely to me. So, how could I ever give them to anyone else? You have been kind, trying to live up to your vows, but I release you from them."

"Only God can do that."

Thomas grunted in exasperation. "Then I order you out of my sight." He jerked the door open and motioned me out. This time, after the door shut behind me, the bolt slammed into place. I clenched my fists and repressed a scream of frustration.

Ignacio came out of the chapel. "Is everything well, my lady?"

"Nothing is well!" I snapped, keeping my voice down so Thomas would not hear. "I tried to speak to him, to make him see reason. He told me about his... affliction. I tried to convince him he could still be everything he was born to be. It only ended in an argument. He has locked me out."

Ignacio smiled. "That is excellent work, my lady."

I stared at him blankly. Had his grasp of English failed him? "I have ruined any progress I might have made. I thought we were becoming friends, but now..."

"But do you not see? He does care. If he did not, he would not have become angry. You are both being forced to confront things you do not wish to speak of. It is awkward and makes you angry. But that is a symptom of caring."

"You think so?"

"Of course. Friends, lovers, they disagree and argue sometimes. It is because they are roused to feeling. Thomas has been past feeling for a long time, but now he is angry. Anger can be good. No, the real danger is when one does not care enough to disagree. Or to talk about it."

"Perhaps," I said. "My mother died when I was young, but I remember the way my father looked at her. Like she was... a treasure."

"Your father knew how to love."

"I thought he did until he left me alone."

"He did not die?" Ignacio looked confused.

"He did." I would not share that pain with a man I still had my suspicions about. "And now Thomas has locked me out."

Ignacio shrugged. "He will unlock the door eventually. And then you can talk again."

He patted me on the shoulder and walked away. I supposed he was right. It was not at all how I had imagined a marriage or a partnership, but when Thomas did unlock his door, I would be ready to speak to him again.

# Chapter Fifteen

I went down the next morning for breakfast, but Thomas was already in his study. I ate alone and spent the day—the next several days—following the maids around, failing to follow Sebastian or Ignacio, and watching over my shoulder as I put more of the house in order. 'Twas only a matter of time before someone attacked Thomas or me again, or before Lord Blacknall turned the thumbscrews on Aubrey Hall to force me to help with whatever he planned for Wishwood, and I had no way to defend myself.

I tried to catch Hal or Will in the woods, to confirm or refute my fear that Will might have had something to do with the attacks on Thomas, and to have a chance to talk to their father, but there was no sign of either of them—not even their snares. But Sebastian patrolled the woods on his horse, his sharp eyes on the alert for any villagers venturing close to the house. Or for me trying to leave it.

After three days, I finally arrived at breakfast before Thomas. He snuck down in the pre-dawn grayness and stopped short at seeing me there.

"I don't recall breakfast as part of our marriage vows," he said. "So, why are you doing this?"

"I enjoy your company." I grinned. "At least when you're not being difficult."

"Difficult!" He swung the chair around and sat resting his arms on the back. "I'm not the one always trying to change things!"

I took a deep breath before our exchange turned into another argument. "True, I have wanted to... *improve* things that seemed lacking." He raised an eyebrow, and I hurried on. "I wanted to feel at home here. I have not had a home since my father died," I added quietly.

"Oh." He motioned for Hughes, who had been lurking down the corridor, to bring breakfast. He spoke again when Hughes was out of earshot. "I'm sorry. It was cruel of Blacknall to bring you to this cursed place."

"Wishwood does not seem so bad—just neglected. Why are you so sure 'tis cursed? Is it your epilepsy?"

"Only in part," he said quietly. "It is my family. My mother died young under mysterious circumstances. Her father fled Spain to avoid the Inquisition and died of a pox soon after. It seems my family is not meant to find happiness."

"That's for you to decide, not some supposed curse."

He glanced down. "I don't know."

As we finished breakfast, he stood to open his study, then growled to himself.

He gestured to the door. "What do you make of this?"

At first, I saw nothing amiss, but then I noticed the marks around the lock: light scuffs in the wood and one deep gouge. "Someone was trying to break in."

"Who? Who would do this?"

"Perhaps the same person who's been trying to kill you?"

"But what do they want with my books?"

I laughed. "You don't care if someone murders you, but you don't want them disturbing your library?"

"Precisely." He smiled just a little. "Go ahead, Mistress Spymaster. Tell me what is happening."

"I don't know." I ran my finger over the scuffs again. They were not deep, but they had been made with something sharp. "Sebastian would benefit from having you out of the way, or someone from the village might hold a grudge against you. But what could they want in your study?"

"Money?"

"Do you keep money in there?"

"Nay, but would they know it?"

I frowned. "It seems more personal than money, even if someone thought Wishwood had any. The ruined portraits, the attacks. What if someone was breaking into the room looking for you?"

He sighed. "Very well. Let's say someone is attacking me. Why?"

I turned over the possibilities. "They want Wishwood."

"Sebastian, then?"

"He sneaks about. He gloats. Aye, I think Sebastian is plotting something." I did not mention the chance that he was a highwayman. I needed more proof first.

"Why not just stab me and have done with it?"

"Everyone would suspect him."

“Ah, true.”

“Though… why not just tell people about your affliction?” I asked.

“He wants his inheritance without any taint on the family name.”

I nodded. “It explains why some of his attacks could have harmed either one of us. He does not want an heir.”

Thomas raised an eyebrow, and a flush warmed my face.

“Then you had better watch yourself, too,” Thomas said. “I am going to have a word with my cousin.”

“You’re going to tell him to stop trying to kill you?”

He smiled. “Something like that.”

I hesitated. “He could also have done something to make someone want to harm him. If they made it look like he’s killed you…”

“I understand.”

Thomas strode off. Not long after, raised male voices echoed from the Great Hall. Sebastian stormed up the stairs to confront me in the gallery, where I studied the chessboard.

“Foolish little goose!” He slammed his hand down, and I steadied the pieces. He leaned down. “’Twill serve no one any good to pique my cousin’s curiosity. Everything at Wishwood sits on a knife’s edge, and if you upset it, we will all bleed.”

He strode off. I glared after him then turned my gaze back to the chessboard, retracing my opponent’s moves to guess what he would do next. What could be in Thomas’s study that someone would want, if not Thomas? The missing deed? Sebastian might be interested in that, especially if it let him inherit sooner. I knew Lord Blacknall wanted it.

Then there were the books. Thomas had said they might be considered heretical. A religious fanatic might be interested in destroying them, and in harming Thomas if he suspected him of heresy. That would lead me back to the village, trying to chase out any zealots.

But what if the books held more than unorthodox doctrines?

❧

"Tell me more about the curse," I said to Thomas the next morning at breakfast.

"Why?"

"I want to help you break it."

He sighed. "I thought you don't believe in curses."

"I don't. But something is hanging over this household. A secret from the past that needs to be resolved."

He chewed a bite of bread, looking thoughtful, then swallowed and shrugged. "My mother is not the first person in my family to be accused of witchcraft or some form of heresy. Her family is from Murcia, in the south of Spain, and rumor says our blood is mixed with Moors, Jews, possibly even gypsies. And so was our faith. The Inquisition tortured many people in her family."

My skin went cold. Dissenters often suffered in England, too, but not like those whom the Inquisition forced into confessions.

Thomas took a deep breath. "There are also stories that some of these ancestors of mine experienced diabolical transformations."

"Transformations?"

"Turning into animals."

"Like the owl."

"Aye." He leaned forward. "Like the owl. Those of the family who were not accused became very devout. They especially favor St. Patrick."

"The Irish saint?"

Thomas smiled. "Murcia is building a great cathedral to honor him because he helped the Christians there defeat the Moors on his saint day. It is also said he once transformed himself and his companions into deer to escape from the notice of enemy soldiers."

I set my spoon down. "That explains the odd prayer in the chapel."

"The Deer's Cry. Aye. I was taught to memorize it at a young age." He leaned back in his chair and folded his arms. "Part says, 'I summon to me all these powers against every cruel merciless power that opposes my body and soul. Against incantations of false prophets, against black laws of heathenry, against spells of witches and smiths and wizards. Christ protect me today against poison, against burning, against drowning, against wounding.' My family took the tale and the prayer as a hopeful sign that the stories about their relatives might be an indication of God's favor instead of his wrath."

"But... you don't believe these stories?" If anyone in the village did, I was surprised Thomas had not been attacked sooner.

He held up his hands in a gesture of defeat. "I don't know what to believe. I only know that I have to live under the cloud of my heritage and my affliction."

"I'm sorry." I reached toward his hand, not quite letting myself touch him. "Does anyone outside of your family—and Lord Blacknall—know of your epilepsy? Or of your family's history?"

"If they did, I doubt I would be sitting here. The stories about my mother being a witch are bad enough."

"We need to look deeper. Maybe there's something in your library that would drive someone to murder."

His expression lightened. "I thought we were quite settled that it was Sebastian."

"There is someone blond involved, too, if you'll recall."

"Ah, you then."

"Of course not!"

But Thomas was smiling. I relaxed, pinning my hopes on that hint of amusement in his eyes. Then, his gaze went blank for a moment. He blinked slowly as he came to and shook his head.

"If you cannot cure me, I'm not sure what good all of this will do. If I don't die in an accident or a fall, someone is bound to find out about my condition eventually, and they'll drag me away. Or drag you away."

"We'll not let that happen." I scooted my chair a little closer to his, and our knees bumped under the table. He tensed for a moment then relaxed and allowed the warm pressure of his leg to rest against mine.

"I'm not going anywhere," I said. "And neither are you."

He chuckled dryly. "Oh, aye, 'twill make a great case for my sanity when I hole myself up in my crumbling ruin of a house and shout defiance at the world."

"It will not come to that. If they question you, they will see that you are sane."

"Not if I have one of my absent moments while they are speaking to me. Or my arm jerks. Stress brings out the worst in me. Only a cure will do, and there is not one. I've searched all these books, and they're full of wisdom, but no cures for the falling evil. Blacknall once brought in a priest to exorcise me, but he declared me a hopeless case."

I frowned. "You've had a run of bad luck with priests, but all we need to do is establish your position, and no one will dare question it, especially not with your wife willing to speak in your defense."

"Is she, then?" He met my gaze, and his dark eyes drew me in.

"Of course." I laid my hand over his, and my stomach fluttered at the contact. He did not move away but tensed as if about to run. "Let's find whatever is in Wishwood's past that makes someone want to kill you, and then they will leave you—us—in peace."

Thomas groaned and pulled his hand from mine to rub his eyes. "My past is not that interesting. I've spent all my life at Wishwood."

"It may not be anything you've done. It could be someone else here. Your uncle, perhaps? Might he have enemies?"

Thomas hesitated, looking a little defensive. "He left all that behind in the Spanish Netherlands, and the war has been over for decades."

"Your father or mother?"

"Father was generally well-regarded. Since everyone thought mother was a witch, I suppose she has a long list of enemies. Maybe a witchfinder has come for me."

"They would want to bring you before the court for the reward."

He stood and paced to the display of rapiers in the great hall. "Someone who thought my mother had cursed them and wanted revenge?"

"Possibly." I joined him, trying to turn his attention from the old weapons. "I'm sorry, this must be difficult for you."

He shrugged. "This has been my life. But how could we find who my mother would have offended?"

"I suppose there would be records if any formal complaints were lodged. If it were just rumors... What about the servants? They might know."

"You're welcome to ask them."

"Could *they* have offended anyone?"

"Margaret routinely offends everyone," he said with a dry grin.

I lowered my voice. "Then why do you keep her on?"

"She's willing to stay. Her father was my father's gamekeeper. Like all these portraits and tapestries, she belongs to the house."

"What about Sara?" I asked.

Thomas lowered his eyes. "What about her?"

"Her situation is unusual."

"Don't harass the girl about her situation." Thomas's eyes were serious now. "You may ask her about the past of the house, but leave her past alone."

"She has no one else who might have an interest in her? Someone who might be jealous that you're providing for her?"

"Someone who... Oh, I see what you're hinting at. That scoundrel did not have blond hair, so I think we can safely leave him out of the equation."

"Then I will do what I can to dig into the history of Wishwood. If you will do the same with your books? See if anyone might be willing to go to extreme measures to steal the information in one of them?"

Thomas gave a careless gesture and returned to his study.

❧

The Hugheses would have seen the most of Wishwood's history, but they were not easy to question, between being mostly deaf—at least when it suited them—and always on the move, however slowly. I cornered Mistress Hughes in the kitchen, where she chopped parsnips.

"My husband said he caught a hare," Mistress Hughes said in her crackly voice. "He's so clever, he is, to set snares."

Ha! Taking credit for my work. But this was not the time to argue. "That would be delightful. I suppose you remember a time when Wishwood was home to great feasts?"

"Cannot say that we ever have."

"Uh." I was not even certain she'd heard me correctly. But most family servants loved to boast about their favorite masters. "I suppose the old Master Westwood was popular with the village?"

Mistress Hughes looked shocked. "Now why would he do that?"

Good heavens.

Hughes came stomping in from the gardens, the skinned hare in one hand. He glared and me and smacked the dead animal down on the block in front of me.

"What are you doing in here?"

"I was just asking your wife about Peter Westwood's days. I suppose things were very different then."

"You leave my wife alone!" He shouted, gripping the hare so I was afraid he might swing it at me. "I'll have you know Master Westwood was the best and kindest of masters. Well-loved by everyone. They sent him to the House of Commons. 'Twas only outsiders who've ever been trouble. Lord Blacknall!"

He spat into the fireplace and glared at me, as though I was the summation of every outsider ever to breach the halls of Wishwood, and then he stalked back outside. Very, very slowly.

I let him go. I was unlikely to get more information from him today anyway, having, apparently, insulted him and all of his forbearers by my very existence. But this was interesting.

The stolid, dependable elder Wishwood had served in the House of Commons. Being involved in politics gave him plenty of opportunities to make enemies.

I hurried back to find Thomas, but Sebastian was lurking in the corridor.

"What do you want?" I asked, trying to slip past him.

He caught my elbow. "Why is the silly goose so interested in Peter Westwood?"

"What is it to you?"

"I know his Lord Blacknall wants you to find my uncle's deed. If you do, don't give it to him."

I yanked my arm free from his grip. "Who says I would?"

"Your dear Aubrey Hall. He could crush it, you know. Then, like me, you would have to watch your inheritance crumble."

"Wishwood will never be yours!"

"I don't see an heir growing in your belly." He smirked. "Bring me the deed, and I will sue out your livery when I inherit. You regain Aubrey Hall, I rescue Wishwood from ruins, and we leave his lordship with nothing. Nay, don't answer me yet. Think on it."

He turned back to the great hall. I shivered and rubbed my arms. I did not have to choose between Aubrey Hall and Wishwood. I would see that both Lord Blacknall and Sebastian ended with nothing.

I drew a steadying breath and went to find Thomas in his study.

"'Tis not breakfast time again, is it?" His eyes glittered with humor.

"I have some new ideas." I glanced back at the door. In the past, someone had eavesdropped on our conversation and reported it to Lord Blacknall, and I knew Sebastian was sneaking around. "Will you walk with me?"

"Walk?"

"In the gardens. I find it easier to think when I'm moving."

He hesitated, then shrugged and stood to escort me out of his study. In the great hall, he offered me his arm. I wrapped mine through his, soaking in the warm thrill of having him so close. But I could not count on having him always there to lean on.

Outside, he paused to let the sunlight soak over us.

"I miss this feeling," he said, guiding me to the garden paths.

"Why do you stay inside, then?"

"That is where my work is." He gave me a speculative look and added, "and 'tis safer for me if I have an absent moment. I feel that I don't belong out here in the sunlight."

"Nonsense. Becca would have ordered you to spend more time outdoors years ago."

"Becca?"

"My old nurse. Lord Blacknall has her now at Aubrey Hall."

"A hostage." His humor vanished as quickly as it appeared, anger hardening his eyes.

"Aye." And I would free her, but I had to keep Thomas and myself alive for that. "I've been talking to Mistress Hughes."

"She's so deaf, I suppose that cannot bother her."

I chuckled. "It bothered Hughes, though. I do not know what he thought I said, but he began defending your father and told me that he'd served in the House of Commons. Did you know that?"

Thomas pursed his lips, and I remembered the sweet warmth from when he had pressed them against mine.

"It sounds familiar," he said. "I never thought much about it. Why does it matter?"

I struggled to pull my thoughts away from the strong angle of Thomas's jaw. "Think of all the things the Commons are involved in: debates over money, religion, the character of the king's ministers. There are plenty of opportunities there for your father to have made some enemies."

"Enemies who would come back more than a decade later to kill *me*?"

My shoulders sank. It did sound a bit ridiculous. "There must be a reason."

Thomas watched my face for a moment then sighed. "How would we find out if there is a connection?"

"There might be something in your father's notes. Political secrets."

"I'll watch for it." He sat on a crumbled stone wall and said in a low voice, "I hate to touch my father's papers. I feel like he's still here, in those pages. I do not want to lose that."

I sat beside him and placed my hand on his. "Your father would not want to see you killed."

Thomas nodded and ran his thumb absently over mine, sending goose bumps up my arm. The breeze brushed a strand of hair across his cheek. I stroked it back with my free hand, then ran my fingers down his jawline. He caught my fingers and held them there, his eyes closed and his lips parted.

"Kate," he whispered.

I leaned closer. He opened his eyes and studied my face, gaze lingering on my lips. He shivered and stood, turning his back to me.

"I'll start today on my father's papers."

He strode back to the house, leaving me alone with a lump choking my throat.

# Chapter Sixteen

Thomas avoided me for the next few days. Just as well. He was too distracting. If he was reading about Wishwood's past, I needed to focus on the present.

"Sara?" I called, walking through the gallery.

The beechwood stools sat around the tables in little groups as if in pleasant conversation, and not a mote of dust dared to dim the soft light bouncing off the polished tables. But there was no sign of the raven-haired girl who had set them in order. The more I asked questions about Wishwood, the scarcer Sara became. Now, the house was too quiet.

I paused at the chessboard. My opponent had drawn his rook back out of harm's way. Only a few captured pieces sat beside the board. My queen hid behind a guard of pawns, knight, and bishop, never in danger, but unable to act.

The portraits on the gallery wall looked down on me. I found the sad eyes of Castora Westwood and their silent plea for help. Dim light reflected off the jagged line of my imperfect repair work. The empty spot next to her, where the slashed portrait of Thomas should have hung, accused me: I had made promises to Thomas. To Wishwood. Yet some *wrongness* still breathed through the halls of the house, hot and itchy on the back of my neck, a shadow in the corner of my eye, vanishing when I turned to face it. A curse?

Nonsense.

I moved my knight forward, freeing my queen, then made for the stairs, my petticoats swishing around my ankles. I stopped short on seeing Margaret heading up toward me. Excellent. Sara at least had to see me in the morning and evening to help me dress, but Margaret could hide from me for days.

She paused, and her eyes widened as I approached. She glanced over the edge of the railing as if seeking an escape, but I closed in before she could weigh whether a leap to the floor of the great hall was better than a conversation with me.

"Margaret. I've been meaning to speak to you."

Her countenance drooped as if I'd told her she had to carry me to London on her shoulders. "Now, mistress? Because I... I need to get something from the garden for Cook. For the master's supper. Urgent like."

The gallery was an odd destination, then, but antagonizing her would not help. "I will walk with you."

She scowled and pivoted to follow me down the stairs.

"You have served the Westwood family most of your life, have you not?"

"I suppose."

"Do you remember anyone ever threatening Peter Westwood? Or being angry with him—angry enough to hold a grudge?"

She cut me a distrustful glance and mumbled something.

"What was that, Margaret?"

"Not that I recall, mistress."

"What of the rumors about Wishwood? When did they start?"

"Don't recall that either."

We stopped at the main door, the rush mats of the great hall crunching softly as Margaret shifted from foot to foot.

I made one more sally. "Did you ever hear anything about the missing deed to Wishwood?"

She shrugged one shoulder, then caught my scowl. "Sorry I'm not more help, my lady. Cook keeps me busy, and it seems everything else just flies out of my head." She curtseyed deeply. "But tired as I am, I will spend some time thinking on it tonight instead of going to sleep when my work is done."

I doubted Margaret had an errand in the gardens aside from avoiding me. But she'd said her master liked her to tend them, and I knew *that* master was not Thomas. I opened the door to let her outside, but I did not bother going with her.

Once she had a head start, I slipped out after her. Margaret did head for the gardens. I trailed along, staying behind the bushes as the mud soaked into my slippers. She collected an armful of red-and-white striped Rosa Mundi flowers, then headed back for the house through the chapel door.

Lurking behind, I spotted Ignacio in the chapel. He was polishing the benches that the household rarely used, but he straightened when Margaret stepped inside.

I sank into the shadows to watch.

Margaret held out her offering of roses.

Ignacio's face brightened, and he walked toward her. She tilted her face up to smile at him, her eyes sparkling in a way I had never seen.

"Excellent, *querida amiga*. These will freshen up the room nicely." He took the roses. "White for purity and red for the blood of Christ."

Margaret put a hand on his arm, gazing into his face with emotion more intense than religious devotion. Then she pulled away and hurried outside, her face downcast once again.

Ignacio watched her go, his expression thoughtful and sad. Then, he gently plucked the petals from the roses and sprinkled the fragrant offering over the floor.

A secret romance! So, Ignacio was her unknown master, not Lord Blacknall. And I did not think—did not want to think—that Ignacio would harm his nephew. But perhaps the belief in a family curse kept him apart from Margaret, too. If I put a stop to such nonsense, everyone would be happier.

I backed away then came down the path again, this time with heavier footsteps. I pretended to stop in surprise at seeing Ignacio, who had returned to his polishing. He glanced up at me and smiled.

"You don't often rest," I said.

"I enjoy keeping the chapel clean. It is respectful. I do not want God to think I have forgotten him when he always remembers me."

"Of course." I stepped farther into the room. The rushlights gave off only a faint glow, but they made the room feel warmer than the great hall. Ignacio had been burning rosemary in place of incense, giving the chapel a sharp, pungent scent that woke my memories of going to worship service with my father.

Ignacio, at least, was the one member of Thomas's household who did not seem to mind examining the past. "Did Thomas's parents use the chapel often?"

"*Sí*. My sister, she liked to pray, and Peter Westwood was a devout man."

I slid onto a polished seat. "If your sister was religious, why do you think people might have said..." Did Ignacio know about the rumors?

"That she was a witch?" Ignacio frowned and sat in the row in front of me, half turned so long shadows fell over his face. His eyes stayed fixed on the image of St. Patrick's prayer. "I do not think the people of the village feared her so much. Not while she was alive, at least. She was kind to them, a good mistress."

"But?"

"The accusations started with those visitors who came. Finely dressed men."

"When Peter Westwood served in the House of Commons?"

Ignacio nodded. "He was often away, and we had many guests. Some did not like the Spanish. They questioned Castora's religion."

"She would have been Catholic."

He studied me as if trying to gauge how much he could trust me.

"Your religious convictions are no concern of mine," I said. "Except where they might affect me. Or Thomas."

He sighed. "We both are Catholic, my sister and I, but we kept our practice quiet and attended whatever services Peter held. It was his house."

"But people might know or suspect that you are Catholic and think Thomas is, too. They even murmur against King Charles for seeming too Catholic. And if they cannot lash out at the king, they might at someone less well-protected."

Ignacio glanced up at the crucifix, his face troubled. "But Thomas is not Catholic."

"Would people know that? His vicar does, I suppose, but the people do not see him worship or listen to his Calvinist philosophies. Religious fanatics make dangerous enemies."

Ignacio's brow furrowed, and he gave me a worried look.

"Has anyone tried to harm you?" I asked.

He shook his head. "Never. And my presence is not a secret. You still must ask why him and not me."

"You are more intimidating."

Ignacio tilted his head. "True. The killer is a coward."

"And you are not master of the manor."

"Is it not a worse crime to kill your master than your master's uncle?"

I sighed. "Aye. It is." I thought again of Margaret. "Is... is anyone else in the household Catholic?"

He gave me a sharp look.

"I have no interest in persecuting them for it," I said. "I just wonder where their loyalties lie."

"None of them are Catholic, and they are all loyal to the family. Wishwood is their home. Their shelter. They would not want to see it disrupted."

That was true. Dreamy Sara, pouty Margaret, and the impossible Hugheses: none would fare well under a more exacting master than Thomas.

"The villagers would not be so suspicious if they knew Thomas better," I said. And they might hold clues to Wishwood's secrets.

"That is likely. They loved his father."

I sat up straighter. If I could not find my answers, I would bring them to me. "What if we gave them a chance to know him? Held a feast? St. John's Eve is coming up. A good night to celebrate."

Ignacio raised an eyebrow. "The night when ghosts walk abroad? Thomas will not like that."

I smiled and stood. "I will convince him."

I arranged my curls in the mirror, making certain each lock of hair was perfect as I rehearsed how I would approach Thomas. There was no love lost between him and the villagers, but he was not unreasonable. When I adjusted the same blond curl for the third time, I realized I was just delaying what I needed to do.

I tapped on the study door. "Thomas? May I speak to you?"

Thomas let me in but retreated so the desk with its age-yellowed papers and tomes stood between us. He had several decades-old account books spread out. I was glad that he and not I was assigned the role of reading them.

I cleared my throat. "We might learn more about Wishwood's past if we invited the villagers to the house."

"I thought we were trying to keep them out."

"I was thinking of holding a feast to show them that we are not enemies."

To my surprise, he did not dismiss the idea outright, but leaned back in his chair and tapped his chin. "Are you going to poach a deer to feed them all?"

I smiled. "I'm not sure I'd be able. But a hare or two would be enough to feed the leading men and their wives. 'Tis not too ostentatious when the villagers have little to eat, and it might show them that we don't object to poaching."

Thomas smiled. "You would make an excellent politician."

"I learned from my father. He took his duties in the House of Lords very seriously. We have to think of our responsibilities and how to balance the needs of the people with our own."

Thomas regarded me curiously. "You clearly admired your father yet sound bitter toward him at the same time."

I folded my arms tightly across my chest. "He was a hypocrite."

Thomas raised an eyebrow.

"He..." I took a deep breath. "He died fighting a duel. After all his talk of our duties—putting aside our desires and passions for the sake of our responsibilities..."

"What was the duel over?"

"I don't know. They found his body run through in a popular dueling field..." I squeezed myself tighter, digging my fingers into the flesh of my arms. "Apparently, whatever it was, was more important than his other responsibilities. His... his family."

"Ah," Thomas said softly. "I'm sorry."

"I keep asking myself what I could have done differently to stop him from going." My voice cracked, and my fingernails dug into my skin through the thin wool of my dress. "If I had been a better daughter: more obedient or more clever—"

Thomas stood and planted his hands on the desk. "Nothing we do can change the choices someone else makes."

"True." I drew a deep breath and lowered my arms. "We can only look out for ourselves. My father clearly thought I was old enough to do so, and I have tried." I met his gaze cautiously, afraid he would recoil from the vulnerability I could not keep from my eyes, or mock my weakness. "But I worry for the people at Aubrey Hall. They rely on me. They don't deserve to be at Lord Blacknall's mercy."

"No one does, do they?" Thomas said quietly, retaking his seat. "Very well, you may hold your feast, and I will attempt to be an amiable host. If I have one of my moments..."

"I will cover it for you."

"And if it proves that you're inviting a murderer into the house?"

"We'll be prepared. You can dispatch him. Or your uncle. I cannot imagine even a host of villagers holding their own against him."

His brow furrowed. "Uncle Igancio?"

"Well, aye. After fighting in the Spanish Netherlands... Why are you grinning like that?"

Thomas attempted to squelch the smile that had slowly spread over his face. "You'll have to ask Uncle about his time in the Netherlands. He's usually quiet about it, but you are... well, you are family now."

He held my gaze for a moment, then quickly looked away. "Arrange your feast. I'll tell Hughes to give you space."

# Chapter Seventeen

I snuck out early the next morning, but Sebastian's horse was already missing from the stables. Or he had never returned the night before. Either way, I looked over my shoulder before entering the dreary dimness of the woods. Rocinante was nowhere to be seen, so I walked to the village, stepping softly and peering out from behind trees at each bend in the path. Birds should have sung their dawn song, and Hal should have been out setting his traps, but only Lord Blacknall's workmen broke the early morning stillness.

I scrambled down a ditch and back up, getting a coating of fine brown dust on my hands and gown by the time I strolled into the village. Men headed to the fields with their scythes stopped to stare at me, so I kept my head high. They needed to know Thomas was no lunatic, and neither was his wife.

When I neared the blacksmith shop, Hal ran out to greet me, his eyes wide and his tousled hair streaked with soot.

"You escaped!" he said, taking my hand and guiding me along. "Even with that sour-faced peacock guarding the woods."

I laughed. "Where did you learn to call my husband's cousin a peacock?"

"'Tis what Will says. Pa told us that peacocks are nasty, screeching birds without much use."

"That they are. I was hoping to speak to your father today. Does he have time to see me?"

"I'll ask."

Hal bounded ahead to the blacksmith shop. Will peered out at me with a suspicious frown, but soon a stocky man with a chest and arms like a hundred-year-old oak came to the door of the shop and motioned me over. Master Smithson's face was darkened by years at the forge, but his eyes were bright as he studied my face. He bowed respectfully but not deeply—after all, a smith was an important man in his village.

"Master Smithson." I acknowledged his bow with a tilt of my head. "I am Lady Katherine Westwood. Thank you for meeting with me."

"I'm more than interested to hear what you have to say." Smithson glanced at Hal and back at me.

I sat on a log bench, resting my hand on the corky ridges of the bark. "My husband and I want to host a feast with the leaders of the village. We hope to see Wishwood and the village healed. Master Westwood will not be free from Lord Blacknall until he reaches his majority, but perhaps there is something we can do to improve our lots before that happens."

Behind us, a tree fell with a crash.

"Aye. It is past time." Smithson sat heavily on another log, blowing out his breath as he arranged his legs. He looked like a school pupil at a too-small desk. “Things are not what they were under his father.”

“You knew Peter Westwood?”

“Aye. A fine man.”

“Do you know much about his time in the House of Commons?”

“Some.” Smithson looked up as he remembered. “At the time, I was a bailiff of sorts for him, and he often told me of his plans. He was on his way to doing great things. It killed him when his wife died.”

“I have heard unpleasant things about that time.”

“I imagine you would have. Rumors flew like blackbirds, and some of them still have not settled.”

“You don’t believe Castora Westwood was a witch?”

“She seemed a good Christian woman to me, even if she was foreign.”

I nodded. “Who else in the village might be favorable to hearing what we have to say?”

He gazed over the village. “I can think of half a dozen men who would come to talk. You’ll want the miller and the tavern keeper for certain.”

“Excellent. Would St. John’s Eve suit you all?”

A moment of superstition flashed in his eyes, but he nodded. “It would.”

“Then we will see you there for supper.”

We exchanged our farewells, and I had to stop myself from skipping back to Wishwood. The sun had risen above the trees, and glittering shafts of light broke through the green canopy.

Hoofbeats echoed down the path. Before I could turn, Sebastian cut me off. He leapt down and grabbed my arms, shaking me until I bit my tongue.

"Stupid little goose! What have you been doing in the village?"

I wrenched away and swallowed the coppery taste of blood. "How dare you touch me!"

"You can lord over Wishwood, but do not play high and mighty with me. You are a child meddling with fire, and you are going to get burned—going to see that all of us burn."

He remounted and cantered ahead, leaving me to glare after him. The throb in my tongue spread to my temples, and I walked half-blind back to Wishwood.

❧

At breakfast the next morning, Thomas was absorbed in reading a book of hours.

"Did you find anything?" I asked.

He looked up as though surprised to find me there. "Sorry, I was lost in the past. I may have found something."

"In your father's records?"

"My mother's. She was keeping track of Father's work, though. She mentions Robert Cecil—I guess Father knew him because he helped negotiate the peace treaty between England and Spain."

"Is that why she wrote about him?"

"No. Father was working with him."

I sat back in my chair. "He was not a popular man, Cecil. Powerful, but with many enemies. Spymaster for Queen Elizabeth."

Thomas stared off over my shoulder. "He was a hunchback, you know. Everyone said he must be cursed."

"And yet he became the most powerful man in England before his death," I prodded. "What was your father doing with him?"

"Hmm. I'm not entirely sure. Trying to pass some kind of contract. Something to do with money. People do get vengeful when money is involved."

"True, but he's been dead for a decade. What does that have to do with you?"

"I'm not certain, but these other people might not be dead."

"Who?"

"She never wrote out their names, just single initials. D, B, A, S. Some were Father's allies and others his enemies. It probably meant something to her, and even to my father, but 'tis hard to follow and harder still to make sense of."

I itched to grab the book from him and try my hand at it, but I resisted. "If Cecil dug up secrets about someone and she wrote it down, there might be someone willing to kill for that book. Do not let anyone see it."

"Who, the servants?"

I shrugged, not wanting to admit I was suspicious of everyone.

Thomas gave me a lingering look. "I'm glad you encouraged me to look into this. I feel like I'm getting to know both of them better." He reached across the table to touch my hand.

"I've caught three hares, my lord!" Hughes announced.

Thomas quickly pulled his hand away. I gritted my teeth and wished Hughes to London, or somewhere even farther.

"Excellent." Thomas's face was a mask of indifference once again. I avoided looking at him again. I did not want to see uncaring where, for a moment, there had been something warmer in his eyes.

# Chapter Eighteen

With St. John's Eve fast approaching, I had no time to dwell on Thomas. Sara, Margaret, and I scrubbed our fingers raw to clean up the old table that had been shoved aside in the gallery, but finally, the white wood glowed as if it had always been polished and loved. With Mistress Hughes' stumbling help, we made bread and roasted hares for pies. It would be nothing like the feasts in Peter Westwood's days, but I hoped the villagers would remember it for some time.

As Sara helped me shape the bread, I gave her a teasing smile.

"You'll be able to set up a fine household someday with all this practice."

She smiled shyly. "As soon as my husband returns."

"Your husband?"

"Aye, mistress. Geoffrey. He used to work here, helping Hughes in the fields. He promised me he would marry me, said I was as good as his wife already. I know he'll be back. It has been two years, but Master Thomas says I may stay as long as I like. Geoffrey must have made his fortune by now." Her smile turned dreamy as she flipped the bread over.

I glanced up at Mistress Hughes, who had not heard, and Margaret, who definitely had. She gave an almost imperceptible shake of her head.

I returned a small nod and glanced again at the always-cheerful Sara. Waiting for a man who was not returning. I pounded a lump of dough with unnecessary savagery. So, this was Sara's innocence. She believed herself a wife—or as good as—not realizing the nature of some men. I turned the dough over with a hard thump. Thomas was right. No jealous man would be returning to question his sheltering of Sara. I would protect her innocence, too.

I would protect Wishwood.

The day of the feast arrived. We pulled the table to the great hall and spread clean linen over it. Chicken roasted on a spit alongside the bread and pies warming in the niches of the huge fireplace. Various puddings and custards simmered in their pots, and we glazed walnuts with honey. I'd even found some ripe apricots for a compote. I would have loved a little cinnamon to add, but this struck a fair balance: more food than the villagers would be used to, but not ostentatious.

For once, Thomas and Sebastian seemed in harmony. Both paced through the house with frowns.

"You're inviting trouble," Sebastian said as I headed for the garden to gather fresh flowers.

"Nay, I'm inviting neighbors."

"They are often the same." Sebastian stalked off.

Thomas placed a hand on the small of my back, warm and familiar, as if we were allies. As if we were husband and wife.

"I hate to agree with my cousin," he said, "but I'm still doubtful that this is wise."

"It is the only wise thing we can do. We must convince the village that you are on their side."

"What if the trouble we've been having is because of something else?"

"The curse?"

"Perhaps. Or perhaps just something that we're not seeing. As I read my mother's books, I feel that there's more of the past in our present problems than we understand."

I placed a cautious hand on his arm. "That may be so, but the problems in the village belong in the present, and they must be resolved, too."

He shrugged and let me return to my work.

I found a bundle of fennel hanging over the door to drive off evil spirits on St. John's Eve. I reached up to pull it down, then remembered Aubrey Hall. My father had laughingly hung fennel, saying he enjoyed the scent and what did it hurt to seek a little good fortune? The fennel stayed.

That evening, our guests arrived, having walked up from the village like a pack of hounds approaching a den, not sure if it belonged to a rabbit or a bear. Hal and Will had come with their father. Hal's eyes were bright and he practically skipped along, but Will slouched his shoulders, and his glance darted around Wishwood in skeptical disapproval. Sebastian sneered at the company and tromped upstairs to watch from the gallery.

The tavern keeper, the miller, and the most prosperous farmers—judging by their clothes—with their wives trailed behind the Smithsons. They stepped into the great hall warily. But there was nothing for them to fear. This room was much different from the one I had entered over a month ago as a bride. The windows admitted light, the rush mats were clean, and the scent was baking bread and the sharp freshness of burnt rosemary. Tallow candles lit the great hall.

Thomas greeted the men, and their faces relaxed a little at his calm manner. Their lord was no lunatic. A bit aloof, and young, but a reasonable man.

I guided the way to the table. Thomas and I sat at the head, and the men and their wives arranged themselves on the sides in the social order known and understood best by themselves. Thomas looked at ease, his dark hair falling down to his shoulders and his dark eyes bright in the candlelight. A leader.

He smiled at me, and the whole room seemed brighter.

Sara and Margaret brought out the first dishes. They served Thomas first with a ceramic plate glazed blue over white like the vase from Spain. The rest of us received pewter.

The village leaders sampled their food cautiously. I did not miss the looks that passed between them, but I made a show of eating a little of everything. Soon, the villagers were enjoying it, too. There was chuckling over the hare pies as the men realized Thomas was poaching from his guardian, and the attitude around the table relaxed. Even Will's expression softened. Maybe he finally believed that I had not been lying to him about conditions at Wishwood.

Thomas's wide reading paid off. He spoke easily with the men about barley and peas, the best sheep for meat and wool, and increasing milk production. I engaged the women in small talk and learned more about the conditions in the village.

They continued on as Sara and Margaret brought out the dessert course: oat pudding. Thomas made a face when he tasted his.

"You don't like it?" I whispered.

"It is fine," Thomas said quickly. "Only, a little bitter."

I tasted mine. Hints of honey wove through the sweetness of the oats, eggs, and cream.

"'Tis fine," Thomas said again and took another bite.

As the conversation continued, his arm bumped against mine. At first, I thought he was laughing. Or twitching as he did sometimes at breakfast. But then he jerked hard against me and collapsed to the floor.

The conversation stumbled to a stop. I fell to my knees next to Thomas. His eyes rolled back, and his body tensed then went slack.

"Thomas!"

I felt his chest. Nothing. I looked around for help. The guests sat frozen in place, their eyes now on the drama playing out on the floor.

"Thomas, breathe!"

I shook him, and he groaned and drew a raspy breath.

"Thomas!" I shook him again, and his eyes fluttered open, unfocused.

Then Ignacio lifted Thomas's upper body, and Sebastian ran downstairs to grab his legs.

Sebastian glared at the guests and hissed under his breath, "Get them out."

He and Igancio carried Thomas upstairs. I looked at the startled faces around the room: witnesses to Thomas's fit. I braced my hand on the table, my fingers cold and shaky.

"My husband has taken ill," I said, trying to keep my voice level. "We will talk again later."

The guests were quick to hurry for the doors. Will looked troubled, almost guilty, as he shuffled out. Hal lingered, watching me with concern, but his father gently pushed him for the door.

I rushed up as soon as they were gone. Sebastian stormed downstairs, not even bothering to sneer at me. Thomas's door was bolted shut. I went through my room and found the connecting door unlocked. I pushed it open to see Igancio making the sign of the cross over Thomas and saying a prayer. Not like a family member beseeching God, but with authority in his voice. When he finished, he looked up and saw me. He motioned me back into my room, and I reluctantly obeyed.

He shut the connecting door behind us.

I folded my arms. "You are a priest."

"I am."

"Not a soldier."

"I accompanied the soldiers as a spiritual advisor."

"You could be killed in England. Who else knows?"

"Only Thomas."

I had discovered him, though; someone else might have. At least it was not some imagined curse keeping Ignacio and Margaret apart. My eyes narrowed as the nighttime movements around Wishwood fell into their proper place. "And the people you bring to his chapel for services. How many?"

"Four or five from around the countryside—all members of old Catholic families. No chance of spies. I am not a missionary priest or a Jesuit, but when they asked for the comforts of the sacraments... How could I turn them away?"

It would have been easy, I wanted to say. But I saw by his pained expression that it would not be for him. "What's done is done." I glanced at the closed door. "How is he?"

"You should go see him."

I hesitated. Would he want to see me? "Can he speak?"

"He seems more himself now."

I hurried to Thomas's room and tapped on the door.

"Enter," he called.

I pushed the door open. From Thomas's expression, he had not been expecting me.

"Are you feeling... better?" I asked, shutting the door behind me.

"Better?" Thomas pushed himself up. "You mean better than when I was lying on the ground, unable to breathe? Or better than when my problem was a secret?"

"It still may be. They just think you're unwell."

"It was a mistake, letting anyone come here." He sank back down.

"You cannot hide forever."

Thomas gave me a dark look. "I should not have let *anyone* come here."

My face paled. "Then why did you? Why did you agree to a marriage you find so inconvenient?"

He laughed bitterly. "If I did not, Blacknall threatened to lock me up in a lunatic hospital. I could not let that happen, not when there might be a cure. But I should have let him take me away. Hope is foolish."

I stood, fists clenched. "If you hide from hope, you will always be hiding from happiness too. You did not choose your affliction, but you are choosing your misery."

"At least with misery, I know what to expect." Thomas lowered his voice. "I have never collapsed like that before. Is that not a sign that I do wrong in wishing for happiness? The curse will never allow it."

I thought of the fennel wilting above the door. Useless superstition. "You are only seeing the signs that you're looking for. You made allies of the villagers today. Perhaps *that* is a sign that you are doing right."

Thomas gave me an unreadable look but said nothing else. He let his head sink back against the pillow. I curtseyed and left him alone. I had to deal with the rest of Wishwood.

# Chapter Nineteen

Hughes and the two maids cleared the table, our fine feast and all of our hard work turning cold and going to waste. I went to help them. Hughes scowled at me but did not object. I picked up the bowl from Thomas's seat with his unfinished oat pudding. Had its tasting bitter been a sign he was getting ill?

I sampled the rice pudding and spat it back out. It was terribly bitter. I was surprised he'd been able to eat it at all.

And mine had not tasted like that.

I took the bowl and hurried back upstairs. This time, I entered his room without knocking. Ignacio was there watching over him.

"What now?" Thomas snapped.

I held out the bowl. "You were poisoned."

"Poisoned?" Ignacio asked. "By this?"

"'Tis very bitter. Someone added something. Maybe ground-up apricot pits. Just to Thomas's."

"Who?" Ignacio asked.

I stared into the bowl as if it would give me answers. "It must have been someone who knew about the feast."

"But that was everyone in the house, and everyone in the village," Thomas said. "So, it could have been anyone."

I nodded, remembering Will's sullen looks. "Even the people at the table. We were all talking, and it only would have taken a moment." I narrowed my eyes. "But don't you dare blame this on a curse."

He gave me a hint of a smile. "I would not dream of it."

Thomas stayed in bed for several days, but one morning I came down to find him waiting for me at the table, books spread out in front of him.

"What is this?" I asked.

"Somewhere, I hope the answer to who is trying to kill me."

I nodded and sat next to him. "We'll figure it out." I put my hand on his, and he turned it over to lace his fingers through mine, filling me with warmth.

The front door slammed open, and Sebastian stalked into the room. He gave our clasped hands a narrow look. "Best prepare for more guests."

"Why?" Thomas asked warily, withdrawing his hand from mine.

"Your noble guardian is on his way and in a foul mood."

I glanced at Thomas, but all the openness of his gaze was gone. He slipped the book onto his lap casually and looked down at his plate. Curse Sebastian and curse Lord Blacknall.

We had barely finished our breakfast when Lord Blacknall himself burst through the front door, trailed by his henchman, Gibbs.

"Bandits!" Lord Blacknall said to the room in general.

"Are you accusing us of being bandits?" Thomas asked coolly.

Lord Blacknall gave him a dark look. "I hardly think you have the stomach for it. Katherine, possibly, but I find her safely here and not riding the roads."

"You've been attacked by bandits?" I asked.

"A highwayman! A knave on a white horse."

I stiffened. Was Sebastian borrowing Rocinante for his troublemaking? It would be smarter than using his own mount.

"'Tis a shame no one manages this place better," Thomas said. "You'd think it had been left to fall into wrack and ruin."

Lord Blacknall glowered at him. "No doubt it was one of those rebellious villagers. They'll soon be put in their place."

"Have you not done enough to them?" I asked, standing.

"Not yet, my dear." Lord Blacknall smirked at me.

"Did you come here just to annoy my neighbors?" Thomas asked, leaning back in his chair.

"I came because it sounds like you cannot manage anything on your own." He glanced into Thomas's study, his eyes narrow. "I'll be making sure everything runs smoothly now."

Lord Blacknall stormed out through the kitchen, toward the guest quarters, with Gibbs in tow.

Thomas gave me a veiled look. "Well, Kate, I hope you will not mind if our meals become a bit simpler again? I find nothing encourages vermin like feeding them."

I nodded my approval, but I could not forget that lingering look Lord Blacknall had given the study.

Sebastian sulked upstairs. He glared at me when I entered the gallery. "This is your fault, you know. His lordship would have stayed away if you had not tried to change things."

I raised an eyebrow. "I thought you benefitted at Lord Blacknall's expense.

Sebastian narrowed his eyes. "And what does that mean?"

"You always make certain everything turns to your favor."

Sebastian rose and glowered down at me. "I have done what I had to make my way in the world, but you know nothing of what you speak, cousin. I would be as glad to be rid of his lordship's presence as you would."

Sebastian stalked off to lurk in some other part of the house. I stared after him. If he was the highwayman, I would expect him to be gloating over robbing Lord Blacknall. Unless by doing so he had drawn too much attention to himself, and now he had to lie low. Still, his words and actions did not seem to fit with the cavalier highwayman I had imagined him to be.

Then who was riding Rocinante? Not Ignacio. He had been sincerely surprised to find the gelding's hooves cared for.

A blacksmith's son would know how to trim a horse's hooves. A blacksmith's son who fed the horse treats and who hated the wealthy.

Will.

And Lord Blacknall suspected the villagers. Will could hang for this. Should I warn him, or would it only draw more attention to him?

And what if Will was part of the attacks on Thomas?

I sat by the chessboard. My last move had been a daring one, putting my queen at some risk to threaten my opponent's king. Instead of moving against my queen, though, my opponent had simply moved his king out of danger. I lifted my queen to chase him, then put her back on her square, not certain what my next move should be.

# Chapter Twenty

I snuck downstairs the next morning to find Lord Blacknall and Sebastian eating breakfast with Thomas. My husband looked as though Mistress Hughes had added lemon to his porridge, but Lord Blacknall stirred the lumpy offering with an expression of utter horror. I choked on a giggle. Thomas winked at me and gestured me away with a tilt of his head. I stifled my laughter and tiptoed back upstairs.

The secret stairs in his room let me into the chapel, where I found Ignacio at prayers.

He broke off and stood to greet me as I shut the door.

"Praying for our deliverance?" I asked, glancing toward the great hall.

He grinned. "God sees fit to give us opportunities to increase our patience, but there's no reason we cannot ask him to keep our afflictions short. You are going out?"

"I find Wishwood too crowded this morning, and Thomas has offered himself as the sacrificial lamb to Lord Blacknall. Besides, I'd like to see what the villagers are saying about Thomas."

"Wise."

"Do you think one of them poisoned him?"

"I almost must believe that. How could it be someone here?"

"I hope it is not. Even Sebastian has no desire for this kind of attention. But I will find out who is too angry to care."

He nodded and returned to his prayers. I slipped out the door and searched the grounds until I found Rocinante. The gelding followed me to the stables in exchange for a carrot scrounged from the garden and allowed me to saddle him. We ventured into the mists just beginning to burn off the woods.

As I neared the village, I found Master Smithson examining one of his sons' traps. He gave a start but relaxed when he recognized me.

"Lady Katherine."

"Master Smithson."

I slid down from Rocinante, and the horse nuzzled Smithson, who scratched the horse's mane in return.

"Is your husband well today?" Smithson asked.

I nodded. "Better." I hesitated. "It appears that someone poisoned his food."

Smithson's eyebrows rose. "Poisoned?"

"Added apricot pits to his pudding."

He wrinkled his nose. "Vicious."

"I am sorry to ask, but—"

"Could anyone from the village be responsible? I hope not. I invited them because I thought we could trust them. But they would be fools to do it! Leaving us at Lord Blacknall's mercy."

"You know Lord Blacknall has returned, then."

"Aye. That's why I'm taking down the traps." He settled onto a log. "He's caused a stir in the village."

"The villagers hate him, then?"

"Aye. They may not be fond of Master Westwood, but they know where the heart of their troubles come from."

I nodded and sat across from him. "What do you know of Lord Blacknall?"

"A little." He shrugged. "His family was elevated under the Tudors."

"New nobility." Many of them were opportunists. Not to say my ancestors had not been, but we were more settled in our ways by now.

"He has a strong investment in the success of the king. He makes most of his money through positions he holds because of his connections at court." He glanced at me. "And the buying of wardships."

Taking advantage of the assets of the estates he was supposed to be managing for his wards. "He would not want to see things change, then. I've learned that Thomas's father had a role in some scheme of Robert Cecil's to reform finances."

"The Great Contract. I remember that. Lord Blacknall would have opposed it for certain. It meant to put the king on a regular income and do away with all these little schemes he resorts to in order to earn money."

"Like the selling of wardships."

"That has long upset many of the noble families. The only ones who benefit are the king and those who buy and sell the wardships. Cecil was Master of the Court of Wards, so he stood to lose by giving it up. But the House of Commons clamored for it to end, and in the end, he relented and agreed it would go in exchange for the king's annual income."

“It sounds like a good plan. What happened?”

“Infighting broke the plan apart in the House of Commons. The people who opposed the plan made sure to turn the king against it, and the idea died with Cecil.”

How close we had come, Thomas and I, to being free. Even when we were only infants, Lord Blacknall had been our enemy. I straightened at that thought.

“Lord Blacknall must have disliked Peter Westwood even back then,” I said.

“Aye, they would not have been allies.”

Master Smithson’s forehead wrinkled as he worried over our problems. I hesitated, wondering if I should mention my suspicions about Will. But Smithson either knew and would have to lie to me about it, or he did not and could not control his son’s actions. I stood. “Thank you. You have given me much to think about.”

I rode back through the woods. The trees cast long shadows over the path, as though trying to cling to what was left of the woods before the workmen made their way here and cleared them away. Then the trees would be sailing over the icy ocean and part of His Majesty’s ships, far from Wishwood where they belonged. I shivered and wished I’d brought a warmer cloak.

I guided Rocinante back by a meandering route, watching the villagers from a distance. The huddle of little houses looked tense, ready to snap, under the dismal gray of the smoke from the woods.

# Chapter Twenty-one

The next day, I hid from Lord Blacknall in the kitchen. Mistress Hughes kneaded the dough for the bread and did not look up as I came in. The kitchen was warm with the scent of yeast and the bone broth simmering on the stove.

Sebastian stormed through, letting a cold draft creep by in his wake. He swiveled to face me.

"You!" he said, grabbing my upper arm. "You have thought yourself so clever, scheming and spying." He gave me a shake. I tried to twist away, but his grip hardened, fingers digging into my muscles like iron manacles, tightening. "Now, you will pay the price for your interference."

"What are you talking about?"

He leaned closer until I smelled the stale cider on his breath. His hair was ruffled and his eyes wide. "I tried to warn you. I have only done what I had to do."

A long, wooden spoon thwacked down on Sebastian's head. He released me and turned with a snarl on Mistress Hughes.

She held the spoon to his nose. A shimmering drop of broth hanging on the rim dripped to the floor.

"Out of my kitchen!" she ordered.

Sebastian spat into the fireplace. "The devil take you. Take all of Wishwood!"

He slammed the door, making the herbs hanging over the cutting block jolt. A slow tremble stole down to my hands, and I folded my arms.

Mistress Hughes gave me a baleful glare.

"Now what's the meaning of all this trouble?" She turned back to her pots. "First that Lord Blacknall shouts at me about roasting peasants—or pheasants—not sure which. And then Master Thomas is not feeling well and wants only porridge, and then Lord Blacknall comes storming and yelling as if Master Thomas's illness was my fault. But he's always been hard to please."

"Thomas?" I asked.

"Eh?" She squinted at me.

"Thomas?" I said more loudly.

"Nay, we're all out of that too."

"You said Thomas is trouble?" I shouted.

"I'm not surprised he's in trouble with Lord Blacknall about." She slammed the bread dough onto the table with a resounding thud. "If I'd known what a pox he was going to be, I would have told the old Master Westwood to bar the door to him no matter how he pounded."

"Old Master... You mean while Peter Westwood was still alive? Lord Blacknall came here then?"

"Politics, that was," she rambled on without hearing me. "They'd come and shout and shout at the master, though he'd stay calm as can be. Never budged." She chuckled. "How Lord Blacknall hated him!" Her face fell. "How I hate Lord Blacknall.

The liberties he would take with the girls. My husband tried to watch out for the young females, but we're none of us a match for the likes of Lord Blacknall."

She shook her head and pounded out her frustrations on the dough.

Liberties. That sounded like Lord Blacknall. No wonder Hughes was protective.

I hurried out of the kitchen and knocked on Thomas's study. He did not answer, so I tried the door. Locked.

"Thomas," I hissed against the door. "'Tis Kate. Let me in!"

I waited for a moment, and finally, the bolt slid. I pushed my way in and closed the door behind me.

"If you're looking for a place to hide from Blacknall," Thomas said, "I've already claimed this one."

I shook my head. "A tempting idea, but I've found out something. I think the 'B' in your mother's book stands for Blacknall. The Great Contract that your father was working on with Cecil, one of the things it would have done was to end wardships. Lord Blacknall was opposed to it. If I understand Mistress Hughes right, he even came here to argue with your father about it."

"Interesting." Thomas turned to leaf through the book. "It might explain why Blacknall seems particularly determined to ruin Wishwood. But what does it have to do with me?"

"I still do not know. But I thought knowing that might help you make sense of your mother's book. Have you found anything else from it?"

He shook his head. "But knowing Blacknall was here might help. I'll reread it and see if filling in names helps illuminate anything."

I nodded and glanced back at the door. "Do you know where Sebastian was going this morning?"

"I try not to think about him unless I have to."

"He said we—I—was going to pay. He's planning something desperate."

Thomas closed his book. "I have forgotten: do we believe he's the one trying to kill me or not?"

"I don't know anymore." My voice shook. I took a moment to steady it. "Everything at Wishwood remains just out of my grasp. The harder I try to understand—to hold on—the less it makes sense. Like I'm reaching for mists."

Thomas stood and rested a hand on my arm, sending a pleasant tremor through my chest. "Shall I help you discover what my cousin is plotting?"

I nodded. Thomas gestured for me to go out first. He followed, locking the door behind him.

Lord Blacknall watched us from the gallery above. He was holding something, turning it over and over in his fingers. The queen from the chessboard. He had disrupted my game.

"I taught you to play better than this," Lord Blacknall said. Not to me, but to Thomas. "Why did you not take the queen?"

"It did not please me," Thomas said.

I stared at him. He did not meet my gaze, but his lips quirked in a half-smile.

"You are a fool if you don't play to win." Lord Blacknall clenched his fingers around the piece and turned his back on us, but I still felt his grip growing tighter.

The front door opened, and Sebastian marched in, half-dragging Will along with him. Will's expression was sullen, but when his eyes met mine, he gave up the fight and stood staring down out the floor, his face red.

"The boy Will Smithson, my lord," Sebastian announced. "Brought here, as you requested, to be examined on charges of banditry and theft."

# Chapter Twenty-two

"Nonsense!" I said, stepping between Lord Blacknall and Will. "He is just a child."

Lord Blacknall smiled coldly. "He is old enough to steal a horse and put on a mask to play highwayman."

Guilt radiated from Will's tense posture.

Lord Blacknall pushed me aside and strode up to Will, who was pale but met Lord Blacknall's glare with one of his own.

Lord Blacknall back-handed him, sending Will's head rocking to the side. "He dared to steal from *my* workmen and assault *me* on the highway. I will see that he receives no mercy."

"You are not the lord of the manor!" I said.

"Unless Thomas lives long enough to turn twenty-one, I am."

"The villagers are upset about enclosing the forest, my lord," Sebastian said. "This will cause further unrest."

Lord Blacknall waved a hand. "I leave you to deal with that."

Sebastian frowned. "Even the king has not been able to stop his subjects from rioting over forest enclosures."

"I will be obeyed!" Lord Blacknall turned from Sebastian to sneer at Will. "Lock him in a room. I will turn him over to the courts to be tried and hanged."

"You cannot!" I launched myself at Lord Blacknall, but Thomas grabbed my arm and pulled me back.

"That is not the way," he whispered in my ear.

I glared at Sebastian, but he lowered his head and hauled Will away, entirely Lord Blacknall's creature. "Coward!"

Sebastian looked back. "I have done what was needed to survive, goose. Just as you have."

"That's right," Lord Blacknall said with a smirk at Sebastian's retreating figure. "Remember, I am the master here. I know what is best for Wishwood."

"Only for yourself," I said. "You care nothing for Wishwood."

"Nor do you, little wench," Lord Blacknall said. "You are here for yourself and your lands. Do not forget that."

He stormed out after Sebastian.

I grabbed Thomas's hand. "What are we going to do?"

He looked pained. "I don't know. Perhaps Ignacio will have an idea."

"We cannot simply let Lord Blacknall take Will away."

"I know." Thomas freed his hand from mine and headed for the chapel.

Sara and Margaret watched with wide eyes from the kitchen corridor. I nodded to Sara. "We *are* going to free him. Please go to Master Smithson and tell him what is happening. Tell him I will find a way to save his son."

Sara nodded and dashed off.

Margaret stood watching me with narrow eyes.

“What is it, Margaret?” I snapped.

“Meaning no offense, my lady.” She curtseyed. “I was just trying to see how you’re so different from Lord Blacknall.”

“And what do you mean by that?”

“Nothing, my lady. I’m certain to be wrong. But ’tis hard to see the difference between two outsiders who come to Wishwood thinking they know what’s best for everyone.” She curtseyed deeply. “I only say it because you asked.”

She made a hasty retreat toward the kitchen. Heat lit my skin, and I took a step after her, but a chill followed the flush and stopped me in my tracks.

Was I different from Sebastian and Lord Blacknall? I was not as spiteful, but we all wanted to control Wishwood’s destiny.

I turned and half-stumbled for my room to sit on the edge of my bed. Facing me there were the images of St. Patrick and his men transformed into deer. Because they called on God, not by any power of their own. Was that not the difference between a Christian woman and a witch? One sought to do God’s will, the other sought only her own.

The torn image of Thomas watched me accusingly. I knelt and smoothed the canvas back into place. I had never mended it. I had never asked if he wanted it mended.

A pounding on my door roused me from my contemplation. I smoothed my dress and swung the door open to find Lord Blacknall looming in the corridor. I stepped out and shut the door behind me.

“What is the meaning of this?” I asked.

“How dare you question me? Have you forgotten who I am?” He grabbed my wrist, but I jerked away.

"Hardly. You are the monster who has tormented me these four years."

His face reddened with fury. "What is the meaning of your actions, or inaction?"

"What do you mean?"

"We had an agreement. You would marry Westwood and produce an heir, and I would spare your father's lands."

"I agreed to the marriage, nothing more."

"And the missing deed?"

"What of it?"

"Useless girl! I have reason to believe your marriage is unconsummated, and an unconsummated marriage is invalid. I will have it annulled and marry you to someone else. Someone more profitable. Thomas is of no use to me. I'll lock him away in a hospital for lunatics."

My fingers trembled. "How unfortunate for your plans that the marriage is valid, then."

"What?" Lord Blacknall's eyes narrowed. "That is not what Sebastian tells me."

"*Sebastian* is not the one I'm married to."

He leered. "Remember, I own you. If you have no heir, then there is no reason to spare your estates after all."

He stalked away, leaving me trembling in the dark stone corridor.

"You lied to our guardian," Thomas said from his doorway, his face in shadow.

"You heard?" The whisper scratched my throat.

"I could hardly avoid it." Thomas took my arm—gently—and led me into his chamber, bolting the door behind him. "Why did you lie to him?"

"About what?"

He raised an eyebrow, and I flushed.

"Does it have to be a lie?" I whispered.

"You claimed something that did not happen. I don't know another word for it."

I could tell him something reasonable. That I lied to protect myself. To protect him. But that was not why I did it.

"I don't care what we've done—or not done," I said softly, forcing myself to meet his unreadable gaze. "I want to be your wife."

"I have provided you neither comfort nor passion." He held out his hands almost imploringly. "How could I be a husband?"

"You are my friend. My companion. We work well together. And I have not done everything only for Aubrey Hall. I have come to care for Wishwood. For you."

He shook his head.

I stepped closer. "You think I asked for this? To let you have this... this control over me?"

"I don't even have control of myself. I don't wish to control anyone."

"And I don't wish to care for someone who does not want me. So, neither of us gets what we want."

"Who says I do not want you?" He stepped closer. So close. So warm, his dark eyes bright.

I struggled to find words. "Your actions..."

"The only thing I can control. And choosing to let my family's cursed past die with me."

"Choose to challenge the curse. To change it. We don't have to be tied to the past. We can shape our future."

He studied me warily, a flicker of interest in his eyes. "I have always felt that happiness mocks me. If I trust it—reach for it—it will dissolve and leave me more... more hurt than before. 'Tis easier not to hope than to have hope snatched away."

"Hope is a risky thing," I said. "But if we trusted each other..." I took a deep breath and reached out to him.

He stared at my hand, indecision in his eyes.

Shouting echoed from the great hall outside.

He turned from me to open the door. My breath caught, and I followed him out to the gallery. Hal stood in the great hall, eyes wild, panting.

"Hal!" I called, hurrying past Thomas down the stairs.

"You have to leave, my lady." Hal stepped forward. His gaze darted around the great hall. "Everyone does. My father is trying to hold them off, but they are past reason."

I stopped and grasped the banister. "Hold them off? Who?"

"The villagers. One of the workmen assaulted a boy when he snuck into the woods to poach—"

"The boy, is he hurt?" I trotted farther down the stairs.

"He'll recover." Hal walked forward to meet me. "But the villagers know about Will too. They have had enough. They're marching on Wishwood."

# Chapter Twenty-three

"Marching on..." I glanced up at Thomas, who was walking down the stairs as if in a dream. "What do you mean?"

"They're rioting, my lady. You must leave here." Hal tugged on my hand.

I stared at him. In the distance, a strange, thrilling noise rumbled: the beating of drums. Like an army. I met Thomas's eyes. "We must see the servants to safety."

Thomas nodded so slowly I was not sure if he heard me or was having one of his moments.

Hal's shoulders sank, but he nodded. "I'll help, too."

"No, you go." I gave him a push toward the door. "Get to safety."

"I'll warn Ignacio," Thomas said.

I gathered my skirts and raced toward the kitchen. "Sara! Margaret!"

Sara appeared, wiping her hands on an apron. "My lady?"

I grabbed her shoulders. "Listen carefully. Go to the cottage and get your boy and your mother. Hide in the woods. Nay, do not protest. I know about your arrangement. Do as I say. They are in danger."

Sara paled and ran for the door. I looked up to find Margaret staring at me.

"Ignacio," Margaret said.

I nodded. "Thomas went to warn him. We all must leave here."

Margaret ran for the door. I darted into the kitchen where Mistress Hughes was laboring over the stove, making a dinner we would not enjoy. The old woman's face was at peace, lost in the world of the old and deaf. I forced my hands to steady and put one on her shoulder. She looked up at me.

"Where is your husband?" I asked.

"What's that?"

I resisted the urge to shake the old woman and instead looked in her face and repeated my question. "Your husband?"

"Oh, he's out checking the traps. We'll have rabbit for dinner tonight."

Perhaps. Roasted over a spit in the woods. "I need you to go to him. Stay in the woods. Together."

The old woman stared at me blankly. Her tongue flicked over her lips several times. Then she nodded and toddled outside.

The shouting from the road grew louder, a wave cresting, prepared to crash over Wishwood. Where had Thomas gone? I dashed to his study, but it was locked.

"Thomas!"

"I cannot find Igancio," he called from upstairs. "Or the boy Blacknall locked up."

I ran to meet him on the staircase. "The mob is almost here. We're trapped!"

"I suppose the future is out of our control after all." He flashed a wan smile. "Luckily, I've had years of practice at avoiding unpleasantness." Thomas took my hand and pulled me back up the stairs.

The sparkling clean front windows exploded in a shower of leaden gray glass. I froze in the gallery. Shouts came from the kitchen corridor, too.

"The secret passage," Thomas said. "Come along."

I let him lead me, his fingers strong and warm. We ran for his room and the hidden doorway. The crunch of breaking glass and cracking wood echoed behind us. Thomas's face drew tight with anger, but he said nothing, only led me down the secret stairs. But when we reached the bottom, voices and the sounds of splintering wood rose from the chapel. Thomas pulled me close.

"Calvinists!" He muttered in my ear, his breath warm on my neck. His tone was half bitter and half laughing.

I huddled against him. If the villagers knew about the secret staircase, Thomas and I would be at their mercy. I wrapped my arms around him and listened to the rapid beat of his heart. He returned the embrace, tentatively at first, then holding me fiercely. The pounding in his chest slowed as we stood there in silence, alone in a storm. A strange stillness descended over me, peaceful in spite of the shouts on the other side of the hidden door. I nestled into Thomas's arms and waited for the end, one way or the other.

The sounds outside slowly faded, and an eerie quiet fell over Wishwood.

"Stay here," Thomas whispered, tiptoeing toward the door.

I followed right behind. The door whispered open, and I gasped. Someone had taken an ax or hammer to the pews, knocking chunks of the wooden benches away. The walls were bare, the icon of St. Patrick destroyed or stolen, the image of Christ on the cross splintered and burned. I pressed my hands to my stomach. Thomas groaned quietly and knelt next to the ruined crucifix.

"Monsters," I said.

Thomas shook his head. "They are frightened. Their children are hungry and they feel helpless. These are the trappings of a church that does not seem to care for their body or spirit."

"You *are* a Calvinist," I accused.

He gave me a grim smile and continued on to the great hall. Glass shards lay across the floor, crunching under our boots. Thomas's shoulders tensed when he saw his study. The door was battered down. His books had been torn and stomped on, and his papers lay in an avalanche across the floor. I put a hand softly on his arm.

"This I find harder to forgive," he said quietly. "If they could read, perhaps they would not turn to violence." His voice hardened. "Then again, there was no one to teach them, was there? They were left to take care of themselves."

"Thomas!" Ignacio's voice echoed from the hall above us.

Thomas turned. "Here, *Tío*. We are unharmed."

Ignacio exclaimed in Spanish and rushed down the stairs. "I have looked everywhere for you outside."

"We were trapped in the secret staircase."

Ignacio crossed himself. "But the house is..."

"A ruin," Thomas said.

"I think they have worked out their anger," I said.

"They have torn down the ditches and walls," Ignacio said.

"Good." Thomas nodded. "Let them have their woods again. Let Wishwood crumble to moldering ruins and the forest reclaim it."

I took his hand. "We can live at Aubrey Hall. Take the servants."

His gaze traveled the broken windows and splintered chairs. "You may offer the servants the choice to go with you. I will stay. I know where I belong."

"Then I will stay with you," I said.

He pulled his hand from me and stepped away. "This is a place for cursed things. Not for you."

I recoiled from his rejection, but it stayed hot and writhing in my stomach. "Please... you don't have to choose this."

Ignacio stepped forward. "My nephew, the villagers have taken Sebastian."

Thomas's dull eyes hardened. "Taken him? Why?"

"They were shouting about Lord Blacknall, but they could not find him, so they grabbed Sebastian instead."

A chill raced over me. "Sebastian was his agent. His spy. That's why he was always sneaking off into the woods. Why he did not want me talking to the villagers. He's been working for Lord Blacknall all this time."

"They are very angry," Ignacio said quietly.

Thomas frowned. He gave me a thoughtful look, then turned his back and faced Ignacio. "He is family. I will go."

He left. He left me standing amidst the ruins of Wishwood and everything I had tried to do there.

I fumbled blindly for a broom in the corner and swept around trampled rush mats to gather clinking bits of glass into sharp, glittering piles. I attempted to scoop the glass onto a broken board to move it outside, but the edges sliced my fingers, drawing spots of hot blood onto my skin.

I needed something to stop the bleeding. I picked through a pile of items tossed into the great hall from the other rooms. A dented pot. The majolica vase, shattered. A pair of fine scissors with etched brass handles stuck into a ball of twine.

The same twine tied across the stairs, meant for Thomas or me. And the scissors must have been Sara's: the ones that once belonged to Castora Westwood.

Ignacio caught my arm, breaking my numb horror. "I have been cleaning the chapel."

"That... that is good." It must have hurt him to see it in such a state.

"So much broken. I find the prayer of St. Patrick in the garden, but stuck to the back of it is this paper about the... *cómo se dice?* ... purchase of lands. It says the first Master Westwood bought the lands from the Lord of Greenwich. I thought he must have bought them from the king, no?"

"Show me!"

We hurried to the chapel—no doubt the safest place Thomas's father could find with Lord Blacknall snooping about—and Ignacio handed me the old paper.

I took it. Held too tightly to the delicate document, and a corner of it broke off in my grip and stuck to the spot of blood on my finger. Indeed, the Westwoods had purchased the priory from Henry VIII as Lord of Greenwich, not as the monarch. Unreal. Impossible.

"He's not a ward."

"*Que?*"

"Thomas does not hold his lands in knight-service. That's why Peter Westwood did not worry about wardship—he assumed you would be Thomas's guardian because he held the lands..." How to explain? "His ancestor did buy the lands from the king, but he did not want his heirs to be owned by the crown forever. Sometimes, when the king was desperate for money, he would sell them, not as the king, but through one of his lesser titles as the Lord of Greenwich. It means that the lands came to the Westwoods free of obligation."

"I am Thomas's guardian?"

"Aye! Lord Blacknall either did not know or did not care in his rush to control lands. He had no legal right to do so."

Ignacio grinned. "Then these lands are Thomas's?"

"They are! And so are mine." I resisted the urge to throw the paper into the air in celebration. "We are free—all of us—from Lord Blacknall!"

Thomas was now his own master, and the master of my lands, too. My smile faded. So, he was free to send me back to Aubrey Hall alone. To never see me again.

I held the paper out carefully. "You must keep this safe. 'Tis our only proof."

"I will guard it with my life." Ignacio took the paper with a wide grin. "I must go tell Thomas!"

"Aye, go!"

I walked back toward the great hall and pulled the tattered rush mats outside. That left the floor much cleaner. I could make more mats. Glass and wood could be replaced. Trees could regrow. But no matter how much I organized and planned, I could not change another person's heart.

I carried the broom back to the servants' corridor. Their doors had been smashed open. Clothes spilled over their floors, trampled and kicked about. An odd scent caught my attention outside Margaret's room. Sour and fruity. Like brandy.

No one else was around. I glanced over my shoulder and stepped inside. The scent grew stronger. Under a torn shift, I found a smashed bottle that reeked of liquor. I straightened slowly. The fireplace sat cold, and the ashes had been drawn into a circle around the name *Ignacio*. Under a blanket tossed near the hearth was the body of a dove with its neck wrung and blood on its chest. The stuff of love spells.

But brandy was not for love spells. It was for forgetting sorrows. Or starting fires. Stolen scissors could be used to cut twine for a trap. To slash Thomas's portrait and his shirts.

A blow from behind smashed into my shoulder, knocking me to my hands and knees. I gasped but rolled over in time to see Margaret raising a broken stair rail to hit me again. I scooted back, legs tangling in my dress.

"Margaret! What are you doing?"

Her gaze flicked to Ignacio's name in the fireplace. "Taking control of my destiny. No more subtle tricks."

I dodged a swing of the rail and rolled around to stagger to my feet. "I don't mean to be your enemy. I'm not the one keeping Ignacio from you."

"You are! You and Master Thomas and your wedding and your heir!" She punctuated her shouts with the railing and swung at me again, backing me against the wall. "With both of you gone, nothing will distract Ignacio from me."

I met her crazed eyes. She did not know he was a priest. This was not the time to enlighten her.

She rolled the broken railing in her hands. "No more sick nephews. Sebastian will throw us out, and we will escape this cursed place. Ignacio will finally do what I want him to."

"Oh, Margaret, that's not how love works."

"Quiet!" She lifted the railing again. I dived for a broken stool and whipped it around to knock her off balance. The railing clattered out of her hands, and I lunged for her, tackling her to the ground.

"Well done, Katherine." Lord Blacknall strode into the room. "You've always been a fighter."

# Chapter Twenty-four

Lord Blacknall hauled Margaret to her feet, and she went limp like a cat caught by the scruff of the neck.

I stared at her, full of pity. It did feel like our love should be enough to sway those we cared for, but of course, that was impossible. That was part of caring: being willing to let go of control over the parts of our life that intersect with theirs. Even when it threatened to crush us.

I fixed my gaze on Lord Blacknall. "She was trying to kill Thomas. And I thought it was you."

He laughed. "I have no need to do such a thing. Poor girl is clearly insane. This place was a fitting madhouse, but I suppose now I will have to commit her to some hospital along with Thomas."

"Don't!" I did not know about Margaret, but Thomas did not belong in such a place.

"Oh, but that's what he's chosen for himself. We had an arrangement: produce an heir so that I could retain control of Wishwood after his demise, or I would be rid of him. You see, I don't have to kill him. There are cleaner ways to dispose of him."

"That was your arrangement with him?" I felt sick.

"Yes, and apparently you gave the boy such a disgust of you that he would rather be locked up than consummate the marriage. The Westwoods have always been stubborn. A thorn in my side."

My eyes narrowed.

Lord Blacknall went on, "I hope you do better with your next husband. Maybe this time I'll sell you off to some old lecher who's not picky about his women."

"Never!" I whirled to escape, but he had his henchman Gibbs waiting for me at the front door. "Thomas!" I screamed.

Lord Blacknall laughed. "He's not coming back for you. You are all alone."

I sagged. Of course, I was. As always. No one wanted me. I twisted my head to glare at Lord Blacknall. "You are not Thomas's guardian anymore. You never were."

He gave me a ghastly smile. "Ah, you found the deed, did you? Where was it hidden? The library?"

I stared. "It was you. In Thomas's room. Sneaking around. You were looking for the deed."

"Gibbs and I, every chance I had. That was one task I could not trust to Sebastian. Thank you for finding it for me. We'll destroy it, and it will be forgotten."

I smiled grimly. "You're too late for that. 'Tis gone from here."

"An inconvenience, but I will deal with it. And with you."

He motioned to Gibbs without releasing his hold on Margaret. "We'll take these women to the other side of the house. I'll lock Lady Katherine up until she sees reason."

I dug in my feet, but my boots dragged over the stone floor.

Hughes and Mistress Hughes limped in from the kitchen, staring around at the destruction. Mistress Hughes let out a gasp at the sight of Lord Blacknall and Gibbs hauling Margaret and me along. She grabbed her husband's arm.

"He's doing it again. Meddling with the women."

Hughes stepped in front of his wife, but Lord Blacknall just sneered at them.

"Stay out of the way, hag."

Hughes let out a stream of verbal abuse in defense of his wife, but Lord Blacknall pushed him aside and led us outside through the kitchen. The walkway cast a long shadow over us as we crossed the stable yard and climbed to the other side of the house.

Gibbs shoved me into an old monk's cell and Lord Blacknall slammed and barred the door. A small window beckoned me, but it was a straight drop to the ground. Too far. I rammed myself against the door and only managed to bruise my arm. My shoulder throbbed. I slid down and rested my head against the age-pitted wood.

I could scream, but who would come? Margaret or Will might hear, but they were locked up, too. If they were even at Wishwood still. And if Lord Blacknall captured Thomas?

I paced the confines of my room. There was only a straw-tick mattress in one corner, a worn-out tapestry on the wall, and the small window looking out over the ruins below. I watched, hoping for a glimmer of movement from down there, even the ghostly monk. Though what help he could give me, I did not know.

Trapped.

I walked faster, running my fingers over the rough, cold walls. Trapped, trapped, trapped. Unless I grew wings as they said Castora Westwood had or wanted to join the monk haunting the ruins, I could not escape through the window. I did not have blankets to try tying them together and climbing down, even if that were likely to work, and the tapestry was not long enough for such a trick.

My fingers raked the tapestry on the wall and I paused, my imagination filling in the worn-out portions of the image. A woman locked in a tower and a knight calling up to her. What could he do? Foolish woman, she should know better than to put in trust in some knight to save her. She would be a prisoner forever. Alone.

I tore down the tapestry and shoved it into the fireplace, but it had gone cold. I would do better to wrap up in the mothy old thing to keep warm.

I spread the tapestry on the floor, tracing my fingers over the threads making up the woman's face. The artist had done subtle work, and I could still make out a smile on the woman's face. She looked down on the knight who would never reach her. Perhaps he had never wanted to. She might have just been living in a fantasy, up there in her tower, safe from reality. Waiting to be rescued. She should not have relied on anyone but herself.

Yet she was smiling. I could not remember when I had really smiled, except when talking to Thomas.

Thomas did not want me here. I did not belong to Wishwood. To him. He had turned his back on me and left me alone.

I still had Aubrey Hall. I should forget him. But I did not want to forget those smiles. Or the feel of his fingers on my skin. They had been a glimmer of warmth in what had been a cold life for many years. I drew up my faded memories of Aubrey Hall, but in the harsh light of day, they had grown empty and dim. It was love that had made them bright. Now, I could not go back to the time when Aubrey Hall had been home, and I could not stay at Wishwood.

I buried my face in the crumpled tapestry and let my tears soak into the faded fabric.

# Chapter Twenty-five

By the time Lord Blacknall came back for me, darkness gathered outside the window. I had dried my face and straightened my dress. The cold security of Aubrey Hall was all that was left to me, and I had not forgotten my duty.

Lord Blacknall stepped into the room and shut the door behind him. It groaned on its hinges.

"Are you ready for a reasonable discussion?" he asked.

"I am." My throat was so dry, the words almost stuck there. But this was how I would escape my cell.

"That is good. It would be a shame for your lands to become a ruin like this one."

I was letting everyone who depended on Wishwood down. I was breaking my promise.

Lord Blacknall smiled thinly, his little mustache curling up. "You must be hungry. Join me for some supper."

He stepped back into the corridor, and I followed obediently like a horse too broken to fight its saddle any longer. We walked down the stairs and through the stable, guided by torchlight. Scared of heights. His lordship did not like that path along the walkway.

We went back through the great hall and up to the gallery. Torn paper and hay ripped from mattresses littered the floor. All of the pictures lay on the ground except that of Castora Westwood. Her dark, haunted eyes watched me from the wall. I turned my back on her.

"What is to happen now?" I asked.

"I will have your marriage annulled and arrange another."

"And Wishwood?"

"It is no longer your concern. It never was, though, was it?"

Not at first, but it had become my concern. Thomas, Sara, the villagers, even the Hugheses. I glanced again at Castora Westwood's sad expression. Maybe I did not have to fail Wishwood. I could keep both of my promises.

"I suppose you'll lock Thomas away. That will please Sebastian."

Lord Blacknall narrowed his eyes. "Sebastian?"

"Of course. With Thomas gone and my marriage annulled, Sebastian will inherit. Will he not? And since he's been saving the money you paid him, he'll be able to sue out his livery."

Lord Blacknall stroked his mustache. "Thomas was much less trouble before I threw you in his way. He might be more tractable once you're removed."

I looked away, trying to keep my face neutral. Agreeing to Lord Blacknall's schemes would save Aubrey Hall and Wishwood. It would save Thomas. I was the only one who would suffer.

"Cheer up, naughty girl," Lord Blacknall said. "At least you will soon live in a place where the servants have their wits about them. No one brought up the bread and chicken as I ordered."

As he strode off to scold someone about the missing food, I stood by the table with the broken chessboard. Such a pity. The game with Thomas had been challenging. Unexpected. I knelt and picked up a few pieces from the floor. One or two had been chipped, but they were still recognizable, and most of them seemed to be there.

My fingers brushed something on the chair. A leather-bound book. I flipped it open. It was a woman's handwriting. Castora Westwood. I flipped pages. She spoke of her fear of a visitor to their house. "Lord B." Blacknall, no doubt. And she spoke of a new friend of her husband who came to join them against Lord Blacknall's plans. "Lord A." He was a widower who had just lost his wife and was left with a young daughter named Katherine. Castora wished that she might have a daughter someday, too.

I ran my fingers over the long-dried ink, trying to be sure the words were real. I carefully set the book on the chair again and glanced at the pile of chess pieces I had gathered. The game did not have to be over. I could not control all the pieces, but I could make my moves wisely and maybe win more than just survival.

I pushed the pieces of the cracked chessboard back together and began placing the pieces on their squares.

A line of pawns stood guard.

Thomas's father and mine had been allies. Against Lord Blacknall.

Rooks in the corners.

His grudge against our families must go far back.

The knights and bishops stood close to their king and queen, ready to protect them.

Did Lord Blacknall make it a practice to buy the wardships of all those who crossed him?

The kings go in their places, unable to move far, but the heart of the game.

Not all of his enemies would end up with orphan children. He had been lucky to obtain control of Thomas and me.

The queens were the final pieces. The crown was broken off of my pale-colored queen, but it was not the crown that made her formidable. I placed both the queens on their squares. *Click. Click.*

Lord Blacknall was not the type to leave things to chance.

He stomped back up the stairs with some stale bread and roasted chicken.

"This will have to do." Lord Blacknall set the food on the other table and pulled a chair over, motioning for me to take the seat. I did, arranging my skirts while I stole glances at Lord Blacknall.

He ate, but his gaze drifted to the portrait of Castora Westwood. His eyes held both longing and hate. I picked at my food. Hunger pinched my stomach, but I did not trust anything Lord Blacknall gave me.

Lord Blacknall finished gnawing the flaky crust and brushed the crumbs from his doublet. "Time to return to your room."

I stood and strolled to the chessboard. "Perhaps we could play another game first, my lord?"

He glanced at the portrait of Castora watching over us. I moved my knight forward, jumping the pawns to let him take the field alone.

"I'm not in the mood for games," he growled.

"I thought it was all a game to you."

"Nonsense, silly child. None of this is a game."

“Of course not. In games, you have a chance of losing. You never lose.”

He glanced again at the portrait of Thomas’s mother.

I rested my finger on my crownless queen. “Except Castora Westwood.”

Lord Blacknall turned his eyes back to me, a dangerous hunger in his eyes.

“You could not control her, could you, my lord? So, you try to control the rest of us. But Wishwood and Aubrey Hall cannot be worth the trouble. Not any longer. Let us go.”

“You *will* obey me. All of you will!” He pulled his dagger.

I shoved the table into Lord Blacknall, knocking his breath away, and ran for the walkway.

# Chapter Twenty-six

The wind howled through the walkway openings and battered me, but I stumbled forward in the dim moonlight. From the other side of the building, I could race down to the stables and find Rocinante. I reached the door on the far side of the corridor.

Locked.

I spun to face Lord Blacknall as he stalked down the passageway toward me, dagger in hand.

"Nowhere to run, my dear," he called over the wind. "I need not bother having the marriage annulled. I'll dispose of you and let everyone think you're still locked away here with me as your guardian."

I pressed back against the door, my breathing tight. Should I throw myself off the walkway? Deny Lord Blacknall this last moment of control over my life? I glanced up to find the owl watching me from the shadows. Was that what Castora Westwood had done?

I looked back at Lord Blacknall. "Was it like this last time?"

He paused. "What?"

"When you killed Castora Westwood. Was she trapped here?"

His face darkened. "She should have been mine, but instead she... she sailed over the edge. White. Like a bird. I would have saved her, but she was beyond my reach."

"She did not want to be your pawn."

"She was a foolish woman. Just like you." He walked toward me. "And you are stubborn, like your father." He leered. "I will kill you with the same blade that killed him."

I gasped. "He dueled *you*!"

"I made it look that way. Now, you'll both know the cost of defying me."

Tears blurred my vision. I blinked them away and whirled for the edge of the walkway, Lord Blacknall froze, his expression haunted.

"Lady Kate!" Hal called from below.

I stopped, my hands on the rough stone, and stared down at Hal, who stood watching with his father and Will, torches in their hands.

A dark blur moved behind Lord Blacknall, and he jerked awkwardly, clawing at his shoulder. Ignacio stepped back, holding a sword.

Not Ignacio. It was Thomas with one of the rapiers from the great hall. He had returned.

His first strike had taken Lord Blacknall by surprise. Now, Lord Blacknall whirled and blocked another thrust of the blade with his arm. Thomas tried to slash, but Lord Blacknall pinned the blade against a stone arch and snapped it. Thomas raised the broken rapier to stab him, but Lord Blacknall grabbed his hand, and the two men wrestled over the rapier.

Thomas gave a shove that sent Lord Blacknall stumbling back against the low stone wall. Thomas swung the broken blade but stopped mid-strike, staring blankly.

Not now.

"Thomas!" I screamed, but it did no good.

Lord Blacknall knocked the broken blade aside. I fumbled after it. Lord Blacknall kicked me in the chest, sending me to the stone floor with a stunned grunt. Angry calls came from below, where more of the villagers gathered to watch.

Lord Blacknall grabbed Thomas by the doublet and hauled him around, swinging him headfirst toward the edge. Thomas came to and latched onto Lord Blacknall's arm. The two men froze there, with Thomas half dangling over the emptiness below. By some trick of the moonlight, it almost looked like a faint glow hung over him. White and golden-brown like the feathers of a barn owl. Murmurs rose from the crowd.

"Thomas!" Ignacio yelled from below.

Something moved overhead. The white owl watched the struggle from the rooftop. I looked back at Thomas. Was the curse real? Would he become an owl and fly away too?

"Don't leave me!" I shouted.

Clouds darted over the moon, and the glow disappeared. Thomas thrust upward with the heel of his hand and caught Lord Blacknall under the chin. Lord Blacknall swayed, cradling his jaw. He snarled and swung a punch, connecting with Thomas's eye and sending him rocking back. Lord Blacknall grabbed the discarded rapier and stepped forward.

The owl dived from her perch directly into Lord Blacknall's face. He shrieked and swatted blindly, stumbling against the low wall.

The owl soared past on silent, white wings. Lord Blacknall cried out and reached for her. His balance tipped, and he tumbled with a wail to the stones below. The villagers shouted—in horror or triumph, I could not tell. I quickly looked away.

Thomas winced and reached out a hand for me. I crawled over to him.

"You know," he said, "this really is a dangerous place. Perhaps I shall have it enclosed."

"Are you hurt?"

"Not badly. You?"

I shook my head. "You came back."

"I did."

"I thought you were going to fall."

"So did I. And, for a moment, I thought the family legend was taking hold, and I was going to fly. But I... I wanted a different future." He met my eyes. "Ignacio told me about the will."

I nodded, remembering afresh what Thomas had said just before he left. Wishwood was no place for me. "We're all free, now."

I did not feel free.

Thomas took my hand and placed it over his heart. I stared at him in confusion, and he met my eyes.

"Some things I can never be free from," he said quietly. "Epilepsy especially. But I realized that just because there are some things I cannot control, it does not relieve me from taking responsibility for the things I can control. You taught me that. And, I'm hoping you'll help me learn more. Help me rebuild Wishwood as it ought to be, without the curse."

I stuttered out a chuckle. "I never believed in the curse. Ghosts, though... maybe."

He laughed and stroked my hair, and I nestled into his chest, fitting like I had belonged there all along, warm, safe, and loved. Home.

"I convinced the villagers to set Sebastian free," Thomas said, "and we caught Gibbs trying to sneak Will away. Everyone will be interested to hear what happened at Wishwood."

Ignacio dashed onto the walkway with Sebastian and the villagers behind him. Thomas helped me stand and guided me back to the gallery. There, I gave an abbreviated account of Lord Blacknall's confession, but I stumbled in explaining the events on the walkway.

Master Smithson met my eyes. "He obviously went mad with grief over his sins and threw himself to his death. All of us here can attest to that when the justice of the peace investigates."

The villagers nodded, and I smiled in gratitude.

"We also found one of the maids locked up in a room, ranting to herself," one of the other villagers said. "We left her there."

I glanced from Thomas to Ignacio. There was enough evidence in Margaret's room to have her hung as a witch, or perhaps burned alive for trying to kill her master, but I did not wish that on anyone. "Margaret has suffered a break. She is a danger to herself." I met Thomas's eyes. "And others. We will need to find a safe place for her."

"I see," Thomas said softly.

Ignacio paled, lifting his hand as if to cross himself before resting it on his chest. He pressed his eyes shut, and his lips moved in silent prayer. Thomas took a deep breath and addressed the others.

"There has been enough excitement today. We should all retire for the night and begin repairs tomorrow."

Master Smithson led the crowd out, keeping a firm grip on Will's arm. Ignacio bowed his head and made for the chapel, shutting the door behind him. Thomas watched him go.

"He will blame himself for Margaret," Thomas laced his fingers through mine. "Though it would have been too dangerous to tell her everything."

"And it may not have deterred her. Her mind is unwell."

Thomas sighed. "I have set myself a Herculean task, have I not?"

I rubbed my thumb over his. "There are more than physical repairs to be made, but with time and cooperation, Wishwood will heal."

"I hope you will be here to help me?"

I nodded, and he pulled me close, wrapping an arm around my waist. I melted into his touch. He caressed my jaw, tilting my face to his. Then he pressed his lips to mine, tentative at first, but his kisses quickly grew bolder, and I forgot everything but the sweet-wine headiness of his lips on mine, his arms holding me against him.

He broke off and rested his forehead against mine.

"I take that as agreement?" he asked, his voice husky.

"Most assuredly. My lord."

He gave me a half-smile. "I suppose I will have to get used to being called that."

"At least by me. It is our son who will be the baron."

"It is to be a son, is it?"

"Perhaps a daughter too." That would please Becca. "And no Lord Blacknall to steal them from us." I tightened my grip on his hand. "He caused so much suffering, but at least we can make something good come from it, too."

"Indeed. But I do not believe that he confessed everything to you so easily."

"I began piecing it together after I discovered in your mother's book that our fathers had been allies."

"I don't remember reading that."

I lifted the book from the chair and showed it to him.

He turned it over. "I'd not found this one."

"I wonder where it came from."

"Maybe Ignacio found it. Or one of the mob left it after ransacking my study." He set the book aside with reverent care and took my hands again.

"Maybe," I said.

But I glanced at Castora's portrait. For a moment, I was sure she was smiling at me as Thomas leaned in to kiss me again.

# Epilogue

Aubrey Hall. Its ancient corridors had lost some of the glamour I remembered from my childhood, but as I breathed in its familiar scents of beeswax candles and lavender scattered among the rushes, with the aroma of roasting meat and sweetbreads drifting down from the gallery, I felt as though my mother and father were close again.

The only jarring sight was Sebastian watching across the great hall with his arms folded.

"Welcome home, baroness," Thomas whispered in my ear.

I smiled up at him. "It is your home now, too."

He raised an eyebrow and scanned the paneled walls and finely-carved chairs of the great hall. "I married above my station."

"Of course, you did, my love. Fortune favors you."

He laughed, and the warm sound spilled through me, widening my grin.

Becca hurried forward to greet us, her face all smiles. "My lamb! I was beginning to fear bandits had stopped your coach."

She bypassed an embrace from me to coo over my growing belly.

"You'll have to brave them yourself to be our nurse at Wishwood," I said.

Becca straightened. "Then I will brave them. You would not manage without me."

"I'm sure we would not," Thomas said, winning an approving look from her. He glanced over at where Sebastian watched us. "And how go matters at Aubrey Hall?"

Becca gave a short nod. "He is competent."

"I'm glad—" Thomas broke off, his gaze unfocused.

"I'm glad we're able to put his talents to good use," I finished for him, drawing Becca's attention to me. Someday, she might know Thomas's secret, but it was up to him to decide.

Sebastian came forward and bowed stiffly. "I hope you find all in order?"

Thomas nodded. "Aye, cousin. And I hope you find your position bearable."

Sebastian smirked. "Despite your constraints, it suits me."

He cast a glowering look at my belly, but he had little to complain about. As long as he managed Aubrey Hall wisely, he could live like a lord on the estate and leave Thomas and me to enjoy Wishwood.

Ignacio joined us from his wanderings about the house, and I nodded up to Thomas. "'Tis time."

Sebastian bowed again. "The feast is prepared in the gallery, and the tenants are anxious to meet their new master."

"Then let us go in."

I took Thomas's arm, and we walked upstairs to claim our place at Aubrey Hall.

# Author's notes

Wardships

The issue of wardships was hotly contested in the Renaissance. In the Middle Ages, it had been used by lords to ensure that the lands of their tenants were managed well, but by the 1500s and 1600s, it was sorely abused and often protested. Mothers did not always retain guardianship of their own children if the father died, and guardians could exploit the lands of their wards and even sell their marriage rights. Monarchs retained the practice because they needed the money. The buying and selling of wardships ended during the British Civil War and was never reinstituted.

Bedding the bride

The practice of "bedding the bride" was meant to make sure a marriage was legitimate, though by the 1600s, it consisted of escorting the newly married couple to their room and leaving them alone. Charles I, famous for his devotion to his wife, refused the tradition on his wedding night, but it continued for some time after him.

Suing out livery

Throughout the Renaissance period, heirs who held their land in knight-service from the king or queen had to sue out their liveries when they reached their majority (fourteen or sixteen for females and twenty-one for males) to have their lands and titles recognized. This was a holdover from the Middle Ages when all land belonged to the king to bestow on his vassals, and it continued as a way for the crown to make money. The practice officially ended in 1660 with the reestablishment of Parliament and the monarchy after the British Civil War, when they passed the Tenures Abolition Act.

St. Patrick/The Deer's Cry

The story of St. Patrick turning into a deer is not as famous as him driving the snakes out of Ireland, but it was an important part of lore about the early British saint. The Deer's Cry, or St. Patrick's Breastplate, is a prayer ascribed to the saint and has been set to music in several lovely arrangements. Though St. Patrick is mostly associated with Ireland, Murcia, in Spain, also holds him in reverence since the Battle of Los Alporchones on St. Patrick's Day in 1452. The Colegiata de San Patricio in Lorca, Spain is dedicated to him.

Enclosure riots

The early 1600s saw a number of riots against landholders who enclosed forest land, infringing on the traditional rights of peasants to use the woods. This was just the beginning of several centuries of enclosures that would eventually force peasants off their lands entirely, either pushing them into the growing cities or to immigrate overseas.

Epilepsy

Epilepsy is an often-misunderstood disease, now and in the past, despite being relatively common in people of all ages. Throughout ancient and medieval history, many people believed it was caused by possession by spirits or other supernatural forces. Though the causes of epilepsy are still not fully understood, medical research suggests it stems from (natural but overactive) chemical and electrical activity in the brain. Not all people with epilepsy have dramatic tonic-clonic or "grand mal" seizures. Some have absence seizures (brief moments of unawareness), myoclonic seizures (limb jerks), or other types of seizures. Some outgrow it, some develop it later in life, and others deal with it throughout their lives. Epileptic seizures can cause disruption and rarely even death, but people with epilepsy generally lead as full and productive lives as those without it. To learn more, visit www.epilepsy.com

# Acknowledgments

Many thanks to those who helped me with this book. The Cache Valley Chapter of the League of Utah Writers, UPSSEFW, and the Clandestines provided me with valuable critiques and support. I'm grateful for the thoughtful feedback offered by Dan, Karen, Keri, and Lori. As always, I am grateful to my family. I couldn't do this without them.

# About the Author

E.B. Wheeler attended BYU, majoring in history with an English minor, and earned graduate degrees in history and landscape architecture from Utah State University. She's the award-winning author of *The Haunting of Springett Hall*, Whitney Award finalist *Born to Treason, No Peace with the Dawn* (with Jeffery Bateman), *Yours, Dorothy*, *Letters from the Homefront*, *The Bone Map*, *Bootleggers & Basil,* and *Utah Women: Pioneers, Poets & Politicians*, as well as several short stories, magazine articles, and scripts for educational software programs. In addition to writing, she consults about historic preservation and teaches history. She lives in Utah with her family, pets, and endless piles of laundry. You can find her online at ebwheeler.com

CPSIA information can be obtained
at www.ICGtesting.com
Printed in the USA
LVHW081334020720
659542LV00025B/2439